NATURE'S FURY

Evelyn suddenly heard a sound she could not account for. A rumbling different from the thunder. It came from the mountain above. She gazed up at the gully, perplexed. The sound troubled her. She felt that she should know what it was.

"What that be?" Dega asked.

"Maybe a rock slide high up," Evelyn speculated.

The next instant a roiling, seething wall of water twenty feet high came hurtling around a bend, sweeping away everything before it.

Recent books in the Wilderness series:

For a full listing turn to the back of the book.

WILDERNESS #54:
PURE OF HEART

DAVID THOMPSON

LEISURE BOOKS NEW YORK CITY

Dedicated to Judy, Shane, Josh and Kyndra.
And for Ben...you rock!

A LEISURE BOOK®

December 2007

Published by

Dorchester Publishing Co., Inc.
200 Madison Avenue
New York, NY 10016

ISBN 10: 0-8439-5930-4
ISBN 13: 978-0-8439-5930-7

The name "Leisure Books" and the stylized "L" with design are trademarks of Dorchester Publishing Co., Inc.

Printed in the United States of America.

10 9 8 7 6 5 4 3 2 1

WILDERNESS #54: PURE OF HEART

Prologue

Out of the east, and the dawn, came four riders.

For as far as the eye could see stretched pristine prairie. Shimmering in the bright sunlight, the grass was stirred now and again by a warm breeze. Stirred, too, were the leaves of cottonwood trees that fringed a meandering stream the four riders had been following for the better part of a month.

The riders did not know the name of the stream. They did not even know if it had one. To them, it represented the safest means of reaching the mountains. They need not want for water. Nor for food, since all kinds of animals came to the stream to slake their thirst and fell to the rifles of the four.

The waving grass and stately trees and ribbon of blue were Nature at her finest. The prairie possessed a rich beauty all its own. Here and there wildflowers added splashes of color to its luster.

But the four men did not appreciate such things.

When they gazed out over the shimmering grass, they saw only grass. When they glanced at the cottonwoods, they saw only firewood. When they stared at the gurgling ribbon of blue, they saw only water. Nature's beauty was lost on the four. For them the natural world held no wonder, no allure. It simply *was*. That a wildflower might entrance them was as remote a possibility as the sun and the moon swapping orbits.

The four rode warily. They bristled with weapons: rifles, flintlock pistols, knives. Every so often the last in line would shift in his saddle and scan their back trail with an intensity that spoke of purpose.

All four had slick, greasy hair. All four were unshaven. Their bodies were strangers to soap and water. So, too, were their clothes. None of them gave any thought to the stink or the dirt. To them it was normal, part and parcel of their existence.

In size they varied. The lead rider was short and wiry and had features much like a rat's. The second man was broad of face and body, with muscles on top of muscles. His low forehead and a vacant aspect to his deep-set eyes suggested he was quicker on his feet than between his ears. The third rider was a mulatto. The fourth, the one who kept shifting in the saddle, had unkempt straw-colored hair that poked from under his cap.

They rode in silence. Only the clomp of hooves and creak of leather marked their passage.

The morning came and went. The sun was directly overhead when the leader motioned at the stream and reined his mount in among the trees. Undergrowth was sparse. He came to a halt at the water's edge and announced, "We will stop for a while."

No one objected. The second man dismounted and stretched, iron muscles bulging under his shirt. "I am plumb sick of all this grass," he declared.

The mulatto slid down with agile grace. "A cow would call this heaven, my friend."

"I ain't no dumb cow," the big man responded.

"No, you're just dumb," said the last rider, he of the straw-hued thatch. "All the brains you ever had have leaked out your ears, Graf."

The broad man scowled. His vacant eyes acquired a flinty cast as he said, "I won't warn you again about poking fun at me, Teak. Keep it up and I'll wring your scrawny neck."

"Go ahead and try," Teak taunted with a sinister smirk, his hand dropping to a flintlock.

The mulatto looked from one to the other. Of the four, he was the only one who might be deemed almost handsome. "Again? Can't you ever get along?"

"Who asked you, Mandingo?" Teak snapped. "I'll do as I damn well please, and no half and half is going to tell me different."

The first rider, the leader, was still in the saddle. His ratlike face twisting in anger, he snapped, "How about me, Teak? Can I tell you different?"

The effect was remarkable. Teak blanched and swallowed and held his hands palms-out, saying, "Whatever you want is fine with me, Bodin. Just say it and I'll do it."

"Shut up, then," Bodin said, and the other man promptly did. Shaking his head in disgust, Bodin swung down. "Mandingo has a point. You prod

Graf too much. Graf is sick of it and Mandingo is sick of it and now I am sick of it. You know what that means, don't you?"

Beads of sweat dotted Teak's brow. He nodded, and the sweat trickled lower.

"Good. We have us a long ways to go, and I'll be damned if I'll abide more squabbling." Bodin squatted and dipped a hand in the stream. He sipped noisily, smacked his thin lips, and straightened. His thin nose twitched as he sniffed the air. "Do any of you smell that?"

Graf turned into the breeze. "I smell nothing."

"Me either," Teak said.

Mandingo was sniffing now, too. After a bit he said, "It smells like burning wood to me."

"It *is* burning wood," Bodin said. "Smoke from a campfire, unless I miss my guess."

"Out here?" Teak marveled.

They had crossed the Mississippi River weeks ago. Where most stuck to established trails, they had struck off on their own, deliberately forsaking the relative safety of the known routes for the very real dangers of the unknown. Some would call them mad, but there was a method to it, and that method was called self-preservation.

"It can't be whites," Mandingo said.

"Then it must be Injuns," Graf guessed, and at the mention, all four felt for their weapons and cast nervous looks about the vegetation.

"Whoever they are, they're west of us," Bodin said, since that was the direction the wind was blowing from. "Mandingo and me will go have a look-see. You two stay with the horses."

"You sure that's wise?" Teak asked. "Maybe we

should swing to the south and sneak on by them. I'm not hankering to have my hair lifted."

"And you think I am?"

"Then why run the risk of them spotting you?" Teak argued.

Bodin pointed at the ground. "If they come this way they'll see our tracks and might take it into their heads to come after us. I'd rather that we jump them than they jump us." Hefting his rifle, he jogged off, Mandingo falling into step beside him. When they were out of earshot, Bodin said out of the corner of his mouth, "That damn Teak is more bother than he's worth. He keeps it up, he won't live to set eyes on the Rockies."

"I am not fond of him, either," the mulatto said, "but he's a good shot, and if those who are after us catch up to us, we will have need of his rifle."

"I bet they turned back long ago," Bodin said. "They wouldn't chase us this far."

"Can we take that chance?"

"I reckon not." Bodin glanced at him. "You always give good advice. Those other two are next to worthless."

"I've been on the run a lot longer than you," Mandingo said.

A sound silenced them, the dull ring of metal on metal. Both stopped, puzzlement writ in their expressions. Bodin crooked a finger, crouched, and cautiously advanced until a thicket barred their way. Flattening, he snaked forward.

Soon a campfire appeared off amid the trees. Seated around it were two men. Young, dressed in homespun, clean-shaven and bright-eyed, they watched the third member of their party, a pretty young woman with copper hair who was bent over a pot. She stirred the contents with a large spoon. It was the sound of the spoon bumping the sides of the pot that Bodin and Mandingo had heard. Parked nearby was a canvas-topped wagon. A team of mules and a horse had been picketed where they could graze on the sweet grass.

Mulatto nudged Bodin. "If you were not seeing this too, I would think my eyes play tricks on me."

"There are stupid people, and then there are stupid people," Bodin whispered, a vicious grin showing his delight. "Stay put. I'll test the waters."

"Want me to get the others?"

"There are only three of them, and one a female. If I can't do it by my lonesome, I should take up the plow or become a clerk." Slowly rising, Bodin cradled his rifle in the crook of his elbow, and adopting as friendly a smile as he knew how, he advanced, hollering, "Hallo, the camp!"

Instantly, the young men rose with rifles in their hands, and the young woman dashed around the fire to stand behind them.

"Who's there?" the taller man demanded. "Who is that?"

"Don't shoot, hoss!" Bodin yelled good-naturedly. "I didn't mean to spook you. I'm harmless."

"A white man, by God!" declared the other young man, whose hair was the same color as the woman's.

"White clean through," Bodin said. "If it's red heathens you are afraid of, I haven't struck sign of any in a coon's age."

"Come closer," the tall man said. He had an outthrust chin and a cocky manner. "Let us have a look at you."

"Look all you want," Bodin responded, his smile still in place. "It surprised me considerable, finding you folks so far from any of the trails."

"We're on our way to Texas," the tall pilgrim revealed. "We found this spot a couple of days ago and decided to let our animals rest a spell."

"Texas?" Bodin repeated. "You've missed it by about a thousand miles. Most folks head southwest from Missouri."

The tall man laughed. "No, you don't understand. We were on our way to Oregon Country and got as far as South Pass when we changed our minds."

"You don't say."

Nodding, the tall man said, "It was my Abigail's doing. She has kin in Texas, and it was her wish all along to go there instead of Oregon." He shrugged. "I finally gave in. And before you say anything—yes, I know it would be smarter to stick to the main trail, but we wanted to strike off on our own."

"*You* did, anyway," Abigail said.

The husband lowered his rifle and held out a hand. "Harold Stonebury. This other gent is Chester Morton, Abby's brother."

"I am right pleased to make your acquaintance," Bodin said sincerely. "And may I say how much I admire your grit?"

Harold smugly smiled at his wife. "See, dear? Not everyone is as skittish as you."

Abigail folded her arms. "I still say we should have signed on with other wagons and been led by a pilot."

"Why spend money we don't need to?" Harold rebutted. "What does a pilot do that I can't?"

"That coffee sure smells good," Bodin said.

Harold gestured. "Where are our manners? Have a seat, why don't you, and tell us who you are and what you're doing out here."

"My handle is Rafer Bodin. I hail from Kentucky. The past five years, or thereabouts, I've lived in Arkansas. Now I'm on my way to the Rockies, where I expect to spend a good long while." Bodin leaned his rifle against his leg and accepted a tin cup from Abigail. "Thank you, ma'am."

"You're traveling by your lonesome?" Chester Morton was amazed. "Aren't you the least bit worried about redskins? Or the white renegades we heard tell so much about?"

Bodin patted his rifle. "So long as I have this, I'm not worried. Besides, most Injuns leave us be if we leave them be. As for the renegades, you three don't strike me as cutthroats."

Chester chortled. "You are a caution, mister. I wasn't talking about us. They say that bands of white killers roam these wilds, slaying who they will."

"They said the same about Arkansas," Bodin noted, "but here I am, still breathing." The wagon, he noted, was laden with furniture and other items for their new homestead. The mules were in their prime, the horse a fine sorrel.

"Folks do exaggerate, don't they?" Harold said. "I always thought it couldn't be as bad out here as most everyone claimed. To listen to some people, a body couldn't trust another living soul."

"The hell of it is," Bodin said, setting down the tin cup and drawing both of his flintlocks, "you can't." He cocked the pistol in his right hand and shot Harold Stonebury in the center of the forehead. The heavy-caliber ball burst out the rear of Harold's cranium, spraying hair and bone and blood all over Abigail, who screamed. Chester gaped at his dead brother-in-law, then at his screaming sister, and grabbed for his rifle. But by then Bodin had cocked his other flintlock, and he shot Chester in the temple.

Mandingo came running out of the brush and grinned at the slaughter. "You didn't save any for me."

"There's still her," Bodin said, wagging a pistol at Abigail. "But not until we've had our fun, of course."

"Of course," Mandingo echoed.

Abigail's hands were pressed to her throat, and her eyes were as wide as walnuts. "Dear Lord, no!" she mewed, and turned to flee.

Mandingo was on her before she took two steps. The thud of his rifle butt slamming against her head was quite loud. But he only hit her hard enough to stun her. Standing over her folded form, he turned as Graf and Teak came crashing into the clearing.

"I'll be switched!" Teak exclaimed. "A wagon and a horse and a female, to boot. We must be living right."

"You can take turns with the woman tonight," Bodin said. "We leave in the morning."

Graf licked his thick lips and hitched at his wide belt. "I almost feel sorry for any homesteaders we run across. They'll end up the same as these."

"That they will," Rafer Bodin said. "There are two kinds of people in this world: sheep and wolves. And we are not sheep."

Chapter One

Evelyn King did not understand it.

She did not understand how the world had changed.

It used to be, she woke up every morning, ate breakfast, puttered around doing her chores, and then either helped her mother sew or knit or cure hides, or went for long strolls along the lake or in the woods. Day in and day out, it was always the same—always perfectly ordinary.

Evelyn liked the lake and the woods, and especially the flowers. She liked them in the same way she liked a vivid sunset. She was grateful to live where she did, deep in the heart of the Rockies. She admired the splendor around her. If she were asked to describe it in one word, that word would be *pretty*.

Then a strange thing happened.

The world became *prettier*.

Evelyn could not say exactly when she first noticed the change. Maybe it was the morning she and Dega had watched the sun rise, and never in the almost seventeen years of her existence had a sunrise been so spectacular. Maybe it was the afternoon she and Dega had been up in a high-country meadow, picking columbines and other flowers, and she breathed deep of their fragrance and stretched her arms to the heavens, and never, ever had she felt so alive. Or maybe it had been the night she and Dega stood under the stars, and she was stirred to the depths of her soul by their sparkling brilliance and sheer numbers.

No, Evelyn could not understand the change. It mystified her. It perplexed her. One day the world was perfectly ordinary, and the next it was so very special.

That had been a month ago.

The caw of a raven woke Evelyn, and she lay still in the predawn dark, warm and cozy under the heavy quilt her mother had made. That high up in the mountains, she used the quilt nearly all year long. Nights, even in summer, were brisk, thanks to the wind that howled down off the glacier overlooking their hidden valley deep in the Rockies.

The raven was cawing up a storm.

Evelyn never much liked ravens. They were too noisy, for one thing. For another, once she'd heard a ruckus in a pine and looked up to see a raven raiding the nest of a pair of warblers. The raven was not after the eggs; it was after the hatchlings. As she stared in horror, it had torn the newly hatched young to bits with its beak and gobbled the bits while the frantic parents flew about the nest in despair. But there was nothing they could do. The raven was many times their size. Ever since, Evelyn would as soon shoot a raven as look at it.

Normally when she heard one, she frowned, remembering the poor warblers. But on this particular morning she didn't mind. She had a lot to do and wanted to get up early. The raven had done her a favor.

Evelyn slid out of bed with the quilt wrapped around her and pattered to the doorway. She was the first up. Shuffling to the fireplace, she jabbed at the charred embers with the poker until she uncovered a few that glowed red. She added kindling and soon flames flared. She had been tending the fire for so many years, she could kindle it blindfolded. Firewood was stacked next to the fireplace. She picked several logs and set them in.

Evelyn went to the counter by the window and checked the water bucket. It was empty. One of her chores was to fill it each night before she went to bed, but she was prone to forget. No matter, she thought, and threw the bolt on the front door. Leaving it open, she shuffled toward the lake. Her parents' cabin, like that of her brother and his wife, and that of her father's best friend and his wife, was situated along the shore.

Humming softly, Evelyn was halfway to the water's edge when a guttural grunt brought her to a halt. She glanced to her right and stiffened. Standing out against the backdrop of stars was a large four-legged creature. Larger than a mountain lion but not quite as large as a mountain buffalo, it did not have antlers. A bear, Evelyn guessed. But whether it was a black bear or a grizzly, she could not tell. She hoped it was the former. Black bears usually ran from people. Grizzlies tended to regard humans as meals.

Evelyn realized she had forgotten her rifle and pistols. Her father would be mad if he found out. If he had told her once, he had told her a million times: never venture outdoors without a weapon. "A mistake like that can cost you your life," he repeatedly cautioned.

The grunt was repeated. The creature sniffed noisily, then took several stiff-legged steps toward her. Evelyn tensed to flee. She could not outrun a bear, but she would try to make it inside. If the bear did not charge, if it was more curious than hungry, she might make it. If, if, if, Evelyn thought, and was on the verge of whirling when the creature wheeled and trotted toward the forest. She saw its silhouette clearly now, and giggled at her silliness. Of course it did not have antlers. It was a cow elk. Five feet at the shoulders and weighing between six and seven hundred pounds, cow elk were huge, but they posed no threat.

The underbrush crackling, it vanished into the gloom.

Evelyn walked to the water's edge but did not dip the bucket in. Instead, she followed the shore for another thirty feet, to where a stream fed into the lake. A stream with water so clear and cold and delicious, she had never had any water like it. Her father said it was runoff from the glacier. Another stream, several hundred feet further, did not have the glacier as its source, and the water tasted different. Good, yes, but not as tasty.

Evelyn dipped the bucket in with one hand but had to pull it out with both. When full, it was heavy. She made for the cabin, doing her best not to slosh water over the brim.

She gazed to the north. Her brother's cabin across the lake was still dark. So was Shakespeare McNair's, to the east. McNair had taught her father practically everything he knew about woodlore and survival, and the two were fast friends. She had long been of the opinion that they were more than that, that they were more like a father and son.

Well beyond McNair's cabin, along the edge of the lake, grew ancient forest. The trees were tall and big around; her mother said they had been there for hundreds of years. At the moment they were mired in the ink of night. It prevented Evelyn from seeing the lodge that stood amid them. She sighed in disappointment but was not aware that she sighed, and moments later she closed the cabin door behind her. She threw the bolt and carried the bucket to the counter.

Remembering the fire, Evelyn crossed to the fireplace. The logs had caught and were burning nicely.

Evelyn returned to the counter and took down the flour and a measuring cup. From under the counter she produced a pan. She was as quiet as she could be, but she could not help making a little noise.

"I must be dreaming."

The woman who stood in the doorway of the other bedroom, shrugging into a robe, gazed at Evelyn in disbelief. Long black hair flowed past her slender shoulders. The nightgown she wore under the robe had been bought for her by her husband. The blue beads that decorated it were her touch.

"You're hilarious, Ma," Evelyn said. "Keep at it and you'll be as funny as Zach." Her brother had a penchant for slinging verbal darts at her.

"The fire is lit, you have fetched water, you are making breakfast," Winona King recited, amazed. "Yes, I am definitely dreaming." Her English was impeccable. Unlike her husband, who wrestled with new tongues, Winona was, as Nate liked to say, "a natural-born linguist."

Evelyn began pouring the flour into the measuring cup. "You make it sound like I never do anything around here."

"You must admit, Daughter," Winona said, "that you have never been fond of doing chores."

"Who is?" Evelyn rejoined. "You can't tell me that you *like* all the sewing and mending and cleaning and whatnot you do."

"It has to be done," Winona said. "The fact that I do it out of love for all of you makes it bearable."

"I don't see how," Evelyn said. "Love or not, drudgery is still drudgery." She prepared hotcakes as she talked. "It seems to me the men have the best of it. While they're off hunting and having fun, we women sweep and scrub and sew and cook."

"Fun?" Winona said. "When they might run into a grizzly or a war party at any time? When they stand to lose a lot more than we who stay home cooking and sewing?"

"I still don't think it's fair."

Winona came across the room and opened a drawer to take out silverware. "I imagine you will change your mind once you have a husband of your own."

"If I ever do," Evelyn said. "I'm too young yet to think about tying myself to a man."

A smile curled Winona's lips, but she did not say anything.

"To be honest, I may never marry," Evelyn asserted. "I like my freedom. I like being able to do what I want when I want. And I hate scrubbing floors as much as I hate anything."

"Is Dega aware of your feelings?" Winona said.

Evelyn paused in the act of stirring. Degamawaku had become her best friend in all the world. His family lived in the lodge at the end of the lake. They were from east of the Mississippi River, and had been forced to flee when whites destroyed their village and wiped out their people. "What does he have to do with it?"

"You have been spending a lot of time in his company," Winona noted.

"Oh, please, Ma," Evelyn said, and laughed. "Dega is my friend. Nothing more. He and I like to do things together. Don't make it out to be something it isn't."

"I would never do that, Daughter," Winona said, turning away so Evelyn would not see her grin.

"As a matter of fact, he is coming over here in a bit," Evelyn revealed. "We're going riding."

"This early?"

"The sun will be up by the time we leave," Evelyn said. "I invited him to breakfast first."

"Oh my," Winona said.

"What?"

"Nothing. But if we are having a guest, I should get dressed. And let your father know so he can join us."

Evelyn set down the pan. "I was sort of hoping he and I could eat alone. We won't take long. Then you and Pa can have your own breakfast."

Winona arched an eyebrow. "When were you planning to tell me? When he knocked on the door?"

"Sorry, Ma," Evelyn said. "I should have mentioned it last night, but I plumb forgot." She looked down at herself. "I've got to hurry. I need to get dressed and fetch eggs from the chicken coop and cook the meal."

"Very well, Daughter," Winona said. "Your father and I will honor your request. We will wait for Dega and you to leave before we come out."

Evelyn beamed and went up and gave her mother a hug. "I knew I could count on you, but I wasn't so sure about Pa."

"Your father loves you as dearly as I do," Winona remarked as she walked to the bedroom she shared with her mate. "He will not mind." Entering, she closed the door but left it open a crack in case she should want to peek out. Soft snoring issued from the bed. She waited a bit for her eyes to adjust, then stretched out on her side. "Husband," she whispered.

Nate King did not stir.

"Grizzly Killer," Winona tried again, using the name by which her people, the Shoshones, knew him.

Nate was on his stomach. He was so big he

took up more than half the bed, one arm hanging over the edge to the floor. Slowing raising his head, he looked about them at the dark. "Morning already?"

"No," Winona said. "The sun will not rise for half an hour yet."

"Then why did you wake me?" Nate asked. "Are the Blackfeet attacking?"

"No."

"Did a mountain lion get at the horses?"

"No."

"Did a coyote raid the chicken coop?"

"No."

By then Nate was propped on his elbow and blinking in confusion. "Then what's so blamed important?" He suddenly gave a start as if struck by an idea. His teeth flashed in the gloom and he reached for her.

"Not that, either," Winona said, and swatted his hand.

"Then what?"

"Our daughter is in love."

Nate sighed and plopped his face back onto his pillow. "You woke me up for *that*? Tell me something I don't know."

"Our daughter is in love, but she refuses to admit it," Winona said. "She has invited Dega over for breakfast and requests that you and I stay in bed until they leave."

"The nerve of the hussy," Nate mumbled. "And in our own cabin."

Winona leaned toward him so she could see him better. "I am not so sure I like your tone. You are taking this far too lightly."

Nate shifted so he faced her. "And you, my dear, are making a mountain out of a prairie dog burrow. Yes, she cares for him. We figured that out weeks ago. If you say she loves him, then I believe you. She was bound to fall in love with someone eventually. It's nothing for us to be upset about."

"Do you remember the first time I invited you to my father's lodge for a meal?"

"Sure. Your mother made venison. It was delicious. Your father kept staring at me as if he wanted to lift my hair. So?"

"Do you remember what we did after we ate? When we went out and stood under a blanket together?"

"Of course I remember," Nate said, and chuckled. "You were about the friskiest little vixen this side of—" Stopping, he sat bolt upright. "Dear God! Find my pistols. When Dega knocks on the door, I'll shoot him."

Chapter Two

Well before sunrise, Degamawaku of the Nan-susequa was up and dressed in his green buck-skins. He tightly laced his green moccasins, which came to his knees, and slid the strap of his green pouch across his shoulder and chest. He made sure the bone-handled knife in its green sheath was snug on his hip.

Green was special to the Nansusequa. It was the color of the grass and the leaves, the color of the forest. It was the color his people associated with Manitoa, the nurturer, That Which Was In All Things, the source of all that was and all that had ever been and all that would be. The Nan-susequa dyed their clothes green and their blan-kets green and anything else they could dye, in Manitoa's honor. Green was their world, green was their life.

Dega picked up his lance. On cat's feet he moved toward the lodge entrance. He did not need light to see. He passed his father and

mother, Wakumassee and Tihikanima. He passed
his sisters, Tenikawaku and Mikikawaku, both
bundled in blankets. At the entrance he paused to
look back. His heart swelled with love for the four
people who meant more to him than anything.

They were the last of the Nansusequa. Dega still
could not quite believe it, could not quite accept
that the rest of their tribe had been massacred.
And for what? For the land the Nansusequa had
lived on since the beginning of all things, the land
that had nurtured the Nansusequa and which
they had nurtured in turn. For land that white
men wanted so they could fell the trees for cabins
and barns and scar the soil with their plows.

Only by the grace of Manitoa had Dega and his
family survived. They were all that was left of
their kind. When they were gone, so were the
Nansusequa. The thought filled him with pro-
found sadness.

With a toss of his head, Dega pushed the green
blanket aside and stepped out into the brisk chill
of predawn. He faced to the east and raised his
arms and gave inward thanks to Manitoa for another day of life, as was Nansusequa custom.

The forest was still. The tall trees that grew on
all sides reminded Dega of the forest in which he
had been reared. But this forest was not the same.
The trees were different, the plants that made up
the undergrowth were different, the ground drier.
Still, it was forest, and it was of Manitoa, and all
that came from Manitoa was good, and it was
right to be thankful for all that Manitoa gave.

Dega headed for the rear of the lodge. It was

not as high or as long as the lodge they had lived
in before calamity struck, but it was of the same
shape and pattern, and in the daytime he would
sometimes stare at it and think of all the other
lodges that once made up the Nansusequa village, and all the happy, smiling, peaceful people
who had lived in those lodges, and his sorrow
would be almost more than he could bear.

In a corral were two horses, gifts from Nate
King and Shakespeare McNair. Dega spoke softly
to them, as Nate had taught him to do, and opening the gate, went in. They came to him, the two
of them, and nuzzled him. Dega marveled, as he
had many times, that these powerful creatures
now belonged to his family, to do with as they
pleased. The Nansusequa never owned horses.
There was no need. Maybe if they had, he reflected, more of them might have escaped their
terrible fate on that day.

"Why can I not stop thinking of them?" Dega
said to the dun, his favorite, as he rubbed its neck.
"Will their memory haunt me all my life?" The
answer was yes. Which was as it should be. They
were the last of their kind, the only People of the
Forest who were left, and they must never forget
all those who had come before.

A bridle hung from a post on the gate. Another
gift, this time from Zach King. Dega slid it onto
the dun, then led the horse from the corral and
closed the gate. He swung on bareback and
jabbed his heels. Skirting the lodge, he emerged
from the trees and reined to follow the lake shore.

A breeze fanned his face and stirred his long

hair. He sniffed and smelled the smoke. Coming, no doubt, from the chimney of one of the cabins. He could guess which.

The inky vault of sky was speckled with stars. Far more than Dega ever saw in the night sky when he was younger. He did not know why that should be, and had once asked Nate King. Nate said it was because the air was clearer this high up. Dega wondered, though, if it might not be because the stars were that much nearer.

Dega rode alertly, his lance across his thighs. He must never forget that this land was not as the land of his forefathers. It teemed with animals new to his experience. There were grizzlies to watch out for. The first time he saw one, he had been amazed. Never had he imagined an animal so huge, so formidable. It called to mind tales the elders had told of a time, long ago, when strange and wonderful creatures roamed the land, creatures much larger than those that existed now. Giant cats with teeth as long as knives. Deer with antlers as wide as a canoe was long. An animal as big as a lodge, with a snake for a nose and two white fangs the length of a man's arm.

Dega had been skeptical. He had secretly questioned whether such fantastic creatures ever truly lived. But not now. Not after seeing buffalo and that grizzly. The buffalo fascinated him. With their great humps and curved horns and oddly shaped bodies, they were like something out of that long gone era.

And everything was bigger here than back east. Black bears were larger, deer were larger, even the rabbits were bigger than the rabbits he was accustomed to. Why that should be, he could not fathom.

A splash out on the lake ended Dega's reverie. A fish, no doubt. Although Evelyn had told him there was something else in the lake, something her family caught glimpses of now and then, something huge that left a broad wake when it swam near the surface. Shakespeare McNair was of the opinion it was a giant fish called a sturgeon, but the others were not so sure.

A cabin hove out of the darkness. McNair's. Dega gave it a wide berth so as not to disturb McNair and his wife in their sleep. He liked the old man. Neither NcNair nor the Kings looked down their noses at him and his family, as whites were prone to do. From the beginning, the Kings and McNair had accepted them for who and what they were, and not thought less of them because of it.

Dega had been surprised. He would be the first to admit that after the slaughter of the Nansusequa, he hated whites. Or tried to. But it was not the Nansusequa way to hate. From early childhood the Nansusequa were taught that hatred and envy and greed and violence were poison to Manitoa.

Since Manitoa was in all things, all things were related. The wild things of the forest were brother and sister to the Nansusequa. Even the whites, as strange and different as they were, were part of the great circle of life. Even the whites were nurtured by Manitoa.

Or so the elders had instructed, and so Dega believed until he witnessed the destruction of everyone and everything he held dear.

Small wonder Dega had struggled with hatred of whites for a while. Small wonder he considered all whites as enemies.

Then along came Nate King and Shakespeare McNair. Whites who had Indian wives and who had adopted many Indian ways. White men who regarded red men as equals. Whites who lived as the Nansusequa elders once taught all people should live.

It had been hard for Dega to admit that some whites were good and decent. It had been hard to extend the hand of friendship to those whose kind had wiped most of his kind out of existence.

Ahead loomed another cabin.

Dega drew rein, everything else forgotten in the realization that *she* was near. Light glowed in the window. A shadow flitted across it. Her shadow, he imagined. His mouth went dry, and his palms grew moist. He kneed the dun on and drew rein near the door. He slid down and raised his hand to knock, as he had learned was the white practice, then hesitated.

Degamawaku remembered the first time he set eyes on her. He remembered being struck by her beauty: by her lustrous hair, by her lithe, graceful body, and by her lovely face. But most of all he had been dazzled by her eyes, by those marvelous, extraordinary, incredible eyes of hers. *Green* eyes, the first green eyes he'd ever seen. Green, the special color of the Nansusequa. Green, the color of the nurturer, of Manitoa.

Suddenly the door opened and there stood Evelyn King, wearing a dark blue dress she once told him she made herself, and holding a spoon. She smiled that smile he could not get enough of.

"I heard you ride up. Breakfast is about ready."

Dega returned her smile. For a few moments he was so lost in her loveliness that he could not remember the words he had worked so hard to learn. "Good morning, Evelyn," he said formally, upset that he did not pronounce the words quite as they should be pronounced. But she did not seem to notice.

"I hope you're hungry. I made enough to feed an army."

Entering, Dega looked for her father and mother, but they were not to be seen.

Evelyn noticed his glance and said, "My parents are still in bed. It will just be the two of us."

Dega hid his surprise. Among the Nansusequa it was unthinkable for a young woman to be left alone with a young man. Another family member must always be present.

"Have a seat," Evelyn said. "I'll have your breakfast ready in two shakes of a lamb's tail."

Dega racked his brain, but he did not know what a lamb was. That it must be an animal was obvious or it would not have a tail. But what did shaking it have to do with anything? Sometimes white expressions confounded him no end. Suppressing his nerves, he moved to the chair she had indicated and gingerly sat.

Evelyn was watching and giggled. "You always do that like you're sitting on glass."

Again Dega was confused. On the table in front of him was what whites called a glass. They used it to drink out of. Why anyone would want to sit on one was beyond him. Clearing his throat, he replied, "We not have chairs when I grow up." He was proud he could say all that. The white language was hard to master, and he wanted to be as good at it as she was.

"None of the Indian tribes do, either," Evelyn said while taking plates from a cupboard. "Indians are more like the Romans. In one of Pa's books, it says that they liked to lie on robes and blankets and such."

Yet more puzzlement. Dega had never heard of the Romans. Were they a tribe of whites? Did the whites even have tribes? He did know about books, though, and glanced at the shelves that lined one wall. The shelves held dozens of books that belonged to Nate King. Nate had explained how the marks on the pages formed words that could be understood just like speech, and had tried to teach him how to read some of them.

"You are hungry, aren't you?" Evelyn asked.

"I am much hungry," Dega assured her. He had not eaten last night just so he could do her cooking justice. It was the first meal she had offered to make for him. Among the Nansequa, when an unattached woman did that for an unattached man, it was a sign the woman was fond of the man. His sister Teni had jokingly said that Evelyn must want to become a Nansusequa. But there was no telling with whites. To them, cooking for a man might only mean, well, cooking for a man. An act of friendship and nothing more.

"Good." Evelyn beamed as she brought over a plate and set it in front of him. She set another down across from him and moved to the counter where a tray and bowls were heaped with food. "I just hope you like what I cooked. I didn't think to ask if there was something special you might want."

"Any food you make, I like," Dega responded.

"Don't say that until you have tasted it. My brother says I'm the worst cook on the planet."

"Zach say that?" Dega could not get used to how the two were always sniping at each other. He liked to tease his sisters and they liked to tease him, but their teasing was not like the teasing between Evelyn and Zach. The teasing they did went far beyond anything a Nansusequa would stand for. Zach said things to her that would have Dega's sisters in tears, and she said things to Zach that would hurt Dega's feelings if she said them to him.

"He's just jealous because he can't cook worth a lick," Evelyn was saying. "His idea of a fine meal is a chunk of half-cooked deer meat."

Dega squirmed in his chair. His own idea of a fine meal was the same. Did that mean she would not like him as much? He felt he had to say something, so he offered, "I like deer meat."

"I like it too," Evelyn said, "but if that was all we ever ate, eating would get mighty boring, don't you think?" Smiling, she came over with the first of the dishes she had prepared. One by one she placed each in the center of the table, then stepped back. "What are you waiting for? Dig in."

Dega was unsure where to begin digging. None of the food was familiar. On a long wooden tray were stacked large circles of what looked to be baked dough. In a bowl were cakes made of cornmeal. In another bowl was some sort of mush. In yet a third were balls of dough of an unappetizing pale hue, as if they had not been cooked or baked long enough. "A lot of food," he said.

"Never let it be said I starved you," Evelyn said. "I recommend the flapjacks to start. The dumplings are for dessert."

"Flapjacks," Dega said. Another new word. But which were they? He was certain they were not the cakes; he had eaten them before. That left the circles of dough, the balls of dough, and the mush. Reaching out, he touched the bowl that contained the latter.

"I trust you like your oatmeal nice and hot," Evelyn said, sliding into her chair. "I added extra sugar."

"Oatmeal," Dega said. That meant one of the others must be the flapjacks. Since the first part of the word, *flap*, sounded a lot like another word he knew, *flat*, and since the circles were flatter than the balls, he took a chance and reached for one. He froze when Evelyn coughed.

"You might want to use your fork."

Dega looked down. Three objects were arranged in a row. The spoon and the knife he recognized, which told him the fork must be the third. Gripping it in his fist, he speared a flapjack and started to lift it onto his plate. To his dismay, the flapjack broke into pieces and fell on the table. "I be sorry!" he declared, appalled by his blunder.

"It's perfectly all right," Evelyn responded. "I forgot to warn you to be careful."

Dega began to gather up the pieces. He hoped it was not an omen of how their day would be.

Chapter Three

The five Crows were on their way to Bent's Fort to trade. They had been traveling for fifteen days and were almost through the foothills. They were in no hurry.

Once a year Spotted Wolf and his wife, Buffalo Calf Woman, made the trip. This year they were joined by Tall Bull and his wife, Owl Woman, and by their son, a youth who had barely seen twelve winters, Tangle Hair.

They expected no trouble. For most of the way they were in Crow country, and the vicinity of the trading post was considered neutral ground. Enemies must bury old animosities or have their tribe banned from trading. Since no tribe wanted that, the truce held. The whites had many marvelous and rare goods, items the Crows and others could get nowhere else.

As usual, Spotted Wolf had a pack horse laden with fine furs. He did not lead the pack horse himself; that was for his woman to do. When they reached Bent's Fort, they would swap the furs for the glittering trinkets his wife loved so much, for a new knife for him, and whatever else struck their fancy.

Tall Bull was a dozen winters younger than Spotted Wolf. In the robust bloom of his manhood, he sat on his horse straight and proud, a bow and quiver slung across his back, a lance in his hand. His wife, Owl Woman, was shy and only spoke when spoken to.

It was the middle of a sunny morning, and before them stretched the vast plain.

Tall Bull, in the course of a conversation with Spotted Wolf, remarked, "I have never trusted the whites as you do. They are not the friends they pretend to be."

"They bring us much we never had," Spotted Wolf said.

"That is no reason to trust them," Tall Bull replied. "They welcome us with smiles only because they want our furs. But there is no warmth in their eyes or in their hearts."

"Are we any different?" Spotted Wolf asked. "We only go to them because we want things from them."

"That is true," Tall Bull conceded.

"I have never said I have great warmth for them in my heart," Spotted Wolf went on. "I have more warmth for the Snakes, who are sometimes our enemies and sometimes our friends. The whites are too strange, their ways too different, for me to ever like them as I do those of my own kind."

"I feel the same."

"The traders mean us no harm. They want only

to trade. That is all we are to them. But I do not mind. Trading with them has given us much we would not have otherwise." Spotted Wolf patted his rifle and touched his steel-bladed knife. "It is worth their fake smiles."

"Soon I will have a rifle," Tall Bull said. He had wanted one ever since Spotted Wolf showed up in their village three summers ago with his. It was the envy of many a warrior.

"The whites give us much that is powerful medicine. They give us much that makes us strong, and we need to be strong to keep our land. The Blackfeet and the Sioux would like it very much if we were weak."

"Fagh!" Tall Bull spat. "Our land has been ours since we took it from the Snakes, and it will go on being ours for as long as the sun endures."

"Would that it were so," Spotted Wolf said wistfully. He shifted to regard the two women and the pack horses. The boy was farther back, half dozing in the heat of the day.

Buffalo Calf Woman said to him, "I want a mirror on a stick like the one Basket Woman has."

Spotted Wolf grinned. His wife had an envious streak that never ceased to amuse him. Whenever she saw something the other women had that she liked and did not own, she had to have one for herself. "A mirror on a stick might cost two furs."

"We have plenty," Buffalo Calf Woman said, letting him know that whatever else they traded for, the mirror on a stick was the item she wanted most.

"Very well. A mirror on a stick for you and bullets and powder for me and after that whatever we find that we like."

Tall Bull waited until they stopped talking to say, "Mirror on a stick?"

"You have not seen Basket Woman's?" Spotted Wolf asked.

"A warrior does not pay attention to what women do."

"A husband should, if only so he can be a better husband," Spotted Wolf said. "The mirror on a stick is in the shape of a face. Glass is on one side, and that shiny metal the whites love so much on the other. Brass, they call it. It has a handle you can hold while you look into the mirror. The women say it is the most wonderful thing."

"Women!" Tall Bull said, and snorted.

"They have their uses," Spotted Wolf said dryly.

"Yes. They cook and they sew and they cure skins and keep our blankets warm at night," Tall Bull allowed. "But if your woman is anything like my woman, she tests your patience."

"Owl Woman gives you cause to complain?"

"All women do. They are not practical. They would rather have silly trifles such as a mirror on a stick than something of greater use such as a rifle or a knife."

"To them a mirror on a stick *is* of great use."

"For what? Brushing their hair and admiring themselves? You would not catch a warrior being so silly."

Spotted Wolf, in fact, knew several warriors who were quite fond of admiring themselves, but he did not mention that.

"Women do so many silly things, it is a wonder we put up with them," Tall Bull declared

"Without them there would be no more Crows."

"What are you saying?" Tall Bull said. "Without cow buffalo there would be no more buffalo. Without cow elk there would be no more elk. I admit females have a purpose, but they need not be so silly about it."

"Talk to me again when you have lived as long as I have," Spotted Wolf told him.

"I will feel the same then as I do now."

"Perhaps," Spotted Wolf said, and smiled.

Suddenly hooves drummed and Tangle Hair came trotting past the women. He pointed to the south in great excitement. "Look! Look! White men!"

Spotted Wolf frowned. He had been so engrossed in his banter with Tall Bull that he had not been as alert as he should be. He had not spotted the four riders angling to intercept them. That they were white was apparent even from a distance.

"Do you think they are friendly?" Tall Bull wondered.

"I do not see why they should not be," Spotted Wolf responded. They were only a few days out of Bent's Fort, and everyone, white and red, respected the long-held neutrality. That, and there had been no trouble between the Crows and the whites in a number of winters. Still, he put his thumb on the hammer of his rifle, and drew rein. "We will wait for them and see what they want."

Tall Bull followed his example, saying over his

shoulder, "You women stay behind us. Tangle Hair, stay close to your mother."

"But, Father," the boy objected. "I am almost a warrior. I should be by your side."

"You have yet to count coup," Tall Bull reminded him. "You will stay with your mother."

The four whites had fanned out and were coming on rapidly. Spotted Wolf was not so sure he liked that. Out of the corner of an eye he noticed Tall Bull nocking an arrow to his bow string. He did not suggest the younger warrior put the arrow back in the quiver.

"They have rifles," Tall Bull mentioned.

"Whites always have rifles," Spotted Wolf said. In and of itself it did not mean anything.

The whites had slowed. Their clothes and their mounts were caked with the dust of many miles. All had greasy hair. Two of them were smiling as if to assure the Crows they were friendly, but there was that about them which filled Spotted Wolf with unease. He thumbed back the hammer on his own rifle.

Tall Bull glanced at him, then held his bow higher so he could unleash a shaft that much faster.

The four whites were approaching at a walk. One had hair the color of the sun. Another was a halfbreed, but not a mix of red and white. White and black, Spotted Wolf suspected, although he had only ever met one black man in his entire life, and thus could not be certain. In the middle was a small man whose features made Spotted Wolf think of a ferret. The man raised a hand in greeting.

"Do you Injuns savvy the white man's tongue?"

"I speak little bit," Spotted Wolf revealed.

"What are you? Shoshones?"

Spotted Wolf's people had another name for that tribe. "We not Snakes. We Crows."

"You don't say," the ferret-man said. "I hear tell your people are almost as friendly as the Snakes or Shoshones or whatever they are."

"Whites no hurt us, we no hurt whites." Spotted Wolf sought to make it clear. He did not like how the broad one was staring at their pack animals, or how the one with the yellow hair was staring at their women. But then, he had to remember they were white men, and many whites had no manners.

"That is good to hear," the ferret-man said. "My name is Bodin, by the way. Might I ask where you're bound?"

"We go Bent's Fort," Spotted Wolf said, pointing to the south.

"We just came from there. Got rid of a wagon and team we did not need." Bodin glanced at the pack horses. "Those are some mighty fine furs you have there, chief."

"I no chief," Spotted Wolf said.

"What kind of furs are they, if you don't mind my asking?"

"Beaver, bear, fox," Spotted Wolf said, and lifted his reins to ride on. He did not like these whites.

"So you are on your way to do some trading of your own," Bodin said. "Those furs should fetch a good price."

"They good furs." Spotted Wolf said.

"We have never met Crows before," Bodin said. "Mind if we ride with you a while?"

Spotted Wolf minded very much. But something—a feeling, intuition—warned him that if he refused, it might anger them, and if he angered them, these four might become violent. Hiding his worry, he smiled and said, "We happy have you ride a ways."

"Good," Bodin said. "That's real good." He grinned at his companions and nodded. The broad one and the breed reined to the other side, while Bodin and the white man with yellow hair stayed where they were. This put Spotted Wolf's party between them. "Off we go."

Spotted Wolf kneed his pinto. "The whites are riding with us," he announced in his own language. "Stay calm and do not give offense."

"I do not like this," Tall Bull declared. "I do not like the faces of these four."

"Neither do I," Spotted Wolf replied. "But they are better armed than we are."

"They stare at our hides," Tall Bull said. "They want them for their own."

"That could be," Spotted Wolf agreed. "You watch the two on your side, and I will watch the two on this side. Tangle Hair, you warn us if they try to shoot us in the back. Buffalo Calf Woman and Owl Woman, be ready to ride for your lives if blood is spilled. Forget the furs. Saving yourselves in more important."

The man called Bodin leaned toward Spotted Wolf. "That is an awful lot of jabbering, chief. What are you going on about?"

"I no chief," Spotted Wolf repeated.

"Sure, sure," Bodin said. "But what were you just talking about?"

"About trading we do," Spotted Wolf lied for only the second time in his entire life. The first time had been when he had seen but ten winters and used his father's knife without permission and broke the tip on a rock. The shame of that lie haunted him for many moons.

"Is that so?" Bodin said. "You must be looking forward to all the things a person could get."

"Hides ours," Spotted Wolf reminded him.

"Whites have a saying," Bodin said. "To the victor go the spoils. Ever hear that one?"

"Me no hear."

"It means that the strong get to take what they want from the weak. Savvy strong and weak, do you?"

Alarm spiked through Spotted Wolf. He should not have let the whites get close to them. Now his wife and his friends were in peril. Unless he could think of something, and quickly, they might lose more than the hides. "Me savvy. Five Crows weak. Twenty Crows strong."

"What's that?" Bodin said. "What did you say?"

Spotted Wolf gestured to the north. "More Crows with us. More families. More warriors."

Bodin straightened and gazed long and hard behind them. "I don't see anyone."

Keeping his voice as calm and casual as he could, Spotted Wolf said, "They get late start. Fall behind."

The man with the yellow hair fidgeted in his saddle. "Do you believe him, Bodin? Could there be more of the red devils?"

"There could be," Bodin said, but he did not sound convinced. "One of us should ride back and have a look-see."

"Nothing doing," said he of the yellow hair. "They might not be as friendly as this bunch."

"I don't care how many there are," the broad one said. "They don't worry me none."

"Why take chances we don't need to?" asked the mulatto.

Bodin appeared to weigh all their comments, and smiled at Spotted Wolf. "I reckon we will push on into the foothills. Thanks for being so hospitable." He slowed, and the other whites did the same. Together they wheeled to the west and departed at a gallop.

Tall Bull grunted. "They are leaving? Good. I do not know how you persuaded them to go, but I am glad you did."

Spotted Wolf was glad, too. But he was also troubled. It seemed to him they had fallen for his ruse much too easily. He gazed after them, then announced, "We should ride faster."

Chapter Four

The Rocky Mountains were Eden all over again.

Oaks grew close to the lake. Cottonwoods lined the streams that fed the lake from on high. Yellow pine was common. As Evelyn and Dega-mawaku climbed, the yellow pine was replaced by somber ranks of lodgepole pines, so named because Indians preferred the tall, straight trees for their lodge poles. Higher still grew glittering stands of aspens. In the fall, those stands became spectacular displays of vivid color.

Evelyn loved the aspens then.

As with the trees, the undergrowth changed with the altitude. Buffalo berry grew near the lake. So did a type of bush Evelyn didn't like because it gave off an odor that reminded her of a skunk. The Indians found a use for it, though, as they did for most everything in the wild. They made baskets from the plant's shoots and a drink from its berries.

Higher up were a few dogwoods and a plant

with pink flowers that Evelyn adored, but for which the whites had no name. There was also a plant that carpeted rocky slopes; its red berries were popular with bears.

A valley so rich with plant life was bound to be rich in animal life. Deer were abundant. Elk, always wary, stayed in deep thickets most of the day, coming out at dusk to forage. On the highest crags dwelled elusive mountain sheep.

Smaller animals were everywhere: ground squirrels, rabbits, pikas, tree squirrels, chipmunks.

Beaver thrived in the streams. Hidden from the outside world in a valley the whites had never discovered and the Indians shunned because they believed it to be bad medicine, the beaver here had not been decimated by trappers. One of Evelyn's favorite pastimes was to watch them at work or swimming about, and to see them slap their flat tails on the water.

Higher up, an occasional marmot would whistle shrilly at their approach and scamper into its burrow. Once they came on a hole with a large mound of dirt at the entrance, which told Evelyn the occupant was a badger. She saw sign where porcupine had indulged their fondness for bark, and trees with slash marks made by roving black bears. Her father said that bears regularly clawed the same tree again and again, marking their territory, as it were, and letting other bears know they were there.

The valley had been home to a grizzly when they arrived. But it had tried to break into the cabin one night, and her father had been forced to slay it.

The avian contingent flourished. On the lake swam ducks and geese and brants. Grouse lived in the bordering brush. Jays with bristly crests shrieked raucously. Magpies often gathered near the water. Woodpeckers went about their business, seemingly ignoring the rest of the world. Evelyn liked to watch them rove up and down a trunk as they pecked and pecked. She always marveled that they pecked so hard, she could hear them from a hundred yards away.

Evelyn adored the songbirds: the robins that warbled near their cabin, the wrens with their tiny cries, the sparrows that frolicked in playful groups, the solitary juncos. Now and then throughout the year Evelyn would spot a bluebird and be ecstatic. She loved birds with bright coloring, loved tanagers and grosbeaks and buntings. But the bluebirds were her favorites. Mainly because, when she was little, her father had told her that bluebirds were a good omen.

Today, as Evelyn climbed steadily higher toward the north end of the valley with Dega following, she smiled in delight when she spied a pair of bluebirds. That she should see them now, when she was so wonderfully happy, was fitting. She pointed them out to Dega and he told her what they were called in Nansusequa. In this manner they had been teaching one another.

For all the splendor, Evelyn was aware there were certain types of animals they did not see, and was glad of it. The meat-eaters were usually abroad in force after dark, which was why she planned to be back at the lake and the safety of their dwellings before the sun went down.

It was still an hour shy of noon, by Evelyn's reckoning, when she shifted in her saddle and suggested they rest a horses a spell.

"As you want," Degamawaku responded, smiling.

Evelyn adored that smile, just as she adored so much about him. She had never met anyone so handsome. Of course, she had never told him that, nor any of her family. It was her little secret. And, too, she was worried that if her brother found out, he would tease her mercilessly.

Drawing rein, Evelyn slid down, her Hawken in her left hand. Around her waist was a leather belt that bulged with two pistols. On her hip hung a knife. She checked that the pistols were snug and moved to a spot where she could see the valley floor, and the lake. The three cabins stood out plain. Over in the trees to the east was the Nansusequa lodge.

"I am glad your family came here," Evelyn remarked. "I like them very much."

"I much happy you like us," Dega said, and inwardly cringed. He knew he had said it wrong. He tried so hard to speak the white tongue as it should be spoken. He was in awe of Evelyn's mother, who learned languages so quickly and readily, it was almost as if they were already in her head. Winona King had known his family but a short while before she spoke Nansusequa amazingly well. He wished he could be like her, to better impress her daughter.

Evelyn perched on a boulder and placed her rifle across her lap. "Do you like it here, Dega? Really and truly like it?"

The question caught Dega off-guard. Of course he did. Why would she even ask? Then he remembered that sometimes her questions were not as they seemed, that she might ask about one thing and want to know about another. "We all like here. My family—" he searched for the word he wanted and nearly whooped with joy when he found it, "grateful your father let us stay."

"You are good people," Evelyn said. "It is awful what happened to the rest of your tribe." She regretted it the instant she said it, for she saw his handsome face cloud with sorrow. "I'm sorry. I should not have brought that up."

"It be all right," Dega said. But it never would. Not as long as he lived. He would never forget that horrible day, never be able to erase from his mind the screams and wails and the blood.

"It *is* all right," Evelyn said.

"Sorry?"

"You asked me to correct your grammar," Evelyn reminded him. "You should say *is* instead of *be*."

"Thank you," Dega said, wilting. He had got it wrong again. To change the subject he gestured at the magnificent vista below. "Your valley much nice." He almost added that so was she.

"It is your valley, now, too. Yours and your family's. It's as much your home as ours."

Dega could not get over how different she and her family were from the whites of New Albion. The Kings and Shakespeare McNair did not hate them because they were red. Even more incredibly, they had been willing to share the bounty of their valley.

How could his family refuse? They had

nowhere else to go. They had lost everyone and everything: their tribe, their lodge, their land. In all the world, they were the last Nansusequa.

Here, they could live unmolested by the outside world. Here, they had friends, the only friends they had. And here was Evelyn. He noticed her staring at him and he coughed and looked away, half afraid she would figure out what he was thinking.

"Are you feeling all right?"

"Yes. Why you ask?"

"You look a little flushed. I hope you are not coming down sick with something."

Once again, Dega tackled the mental task of translating. Coming was what a person did when they walked toward someone else, as when Evelyn's mother would call her and Evelyn would reply, "I am coming." Down was the opposite of up. *Coming down*, then, must mean to go lower. But that made no sense, since they were headed up the mountain, not down it. Then there was the *with something*. With what? He was so confused, he did not know what to say, so he did as he often did when he did not want to appear stupid in her eyes: he looked at her and smiled.

"I guess you are fine," Evelyn said. That smile of his always made her grow warm inside. "Do you ever get sick much? You and your family don't strike me as sickly people."

Dega was near panic-struck. He had forgotten what sick meant. To stall, he resorted to another of his tricks. He repeated what she had said. "Sick?" Whenever he did that, she sometimes would talk more about what had confused him, and in the talking, make her meaning more clear.

"Yes. You know. Sick as in ill. Fever, cough, the chills, those sorts of things. My family has hardly ever been sick. We are a hardy bunch, I guess. My pa says it's because we spend so much time outdoors, and eat well. Back in the States it is different. There, people are cooped up in houses or apartments. They spend all their time inside, either at work or at home. They don't eat as they should, either, and many of them are sickly. I wouldn't want to live like that. Would you?"

Dega hesitated. Clearly, she expected an answer. A yes or a no might do, but which was the right one? If he understood correctly, she had asked if he would want to live like whites who spent all their time in their lodges and rarely ate food. Why they should do either was beyond him, but since neither appealed to him, he answered her honestly. "No."

"I didn't think so," Evelyn said. She gnawed on her lower lip before saying, "It's funny how life works out. There was a time when I could not wait to grow old enough to go live in the States on my own. I wanted nothing more to do with the wilderness. Can you believe that?"

Dega was spared another mental wrestling match. She went on without waiting for a reply.

"I thought civilization had more to offer. Clothes you can buy off the rack and not have to make yourself. Food you can buy at a general store or eat cooked at a restaurant, and not have to shoot it and cook it yourself. Carriages to ride around in. The theater and socials. It was all so grand to me."

"Grand?" Dega said.

"I know, I know. I was kidding myself. I found that out when a woman who hated my family kidnapped me. I told you about that. I learned the hard way that there is a dark side to civilization." Evelyn shuddered, recalling the terror of those times. "I learned, too, that civilized life is not as carefree as I imagined. I guess it is true that we always think the grass is greener on the other side of the fence, but it isn't."

"Fence?"

Evelyn grinned. "Oh, never mind. I'm just prattling. Why don't we keep going? We can be at the cliffs in an hour, and with luck we will see a few mountain sheep."

That was the reason for their outing. The other day she had spotted several high on a cliff to the north, moving specks against the backdrop of rock, and pointed them out to Dega. He then mentioned that he had no idea what they were, as there were no mountain sheep, or mountains, where he grew up.

Evelyn had been quick to propose they ride to the cliffs so he could see them. She mentioned, to be polite, that if he wanted, he could bring his family along, but he said that he doubted they had any interest in making the long ride just to see animals jump around on rocks.

Unknown to Evelyn, Degamawaku had not been entirely truthful. The People of the Forest were keenly interested in all wildlife. To them, animals were not mindless brutes fit only to be slain and eaten, but fellow creatures that existed by virtue of That Which Is In All Things, and as such, worthy of respect.

A cardinal belief of the Nansusequa was that they must always strive to live in harmony with all living things, and to that end, the more they knew about their fellow creatures, the better able they were to achieve harmony.

Dega's family would very much have liked to make the outing to the cliffs—but he never mentioned it to them. He only told them he was going for a ride with Evelyn. He did not mention the mountain sheep because he wanted to be alone with her.

As Dega watched her mount and head on up the slope, riding with that unconscious natural grace she possessed, a constriction formed in his throat. He had to look away for fear she would glance back and read his feelings on his face.

Degamawaku was in love. At least, he thought it was love. He had never been in love before, not this kind of love, so he had nothing to compare it to. He pined for her when they were separated and dreamed of her when he was asleep and saw her face float in the air before him every minute that he was awake.

It scared him.

Dega had always imagined that when he one day fell in love, the woman would be Nansusequa. They would live in the lodge of his father, and raise children together, and life would be as it had always been for him and his people. He never considered marrying a woman not of his tribe, and he never, ever entertained the faintest notion that the woman he would fall in love with would be white.

For weeks now the two of them had spent

nearly all their free time together. They had become fast friends. She was a wonderful companion, easy to talk to, always lively and interesting, and so lovely.

Dega could not say when, exactly, he began to think of her as more than a friend, but one day he woke up after dreaming of her, his skin hot and prickly and his throat dry, and he knew a change had taken place.

"Dega? Are you listening?"

Shocked that Evelyn had spoken to him and he had been too absorbed to notice, Dega glanced up. She had slowed. He promptly did the same. "I be sorry. You speak?"

"I asked if you heard that twig snap," Evelyn said, and pointed at a thicket above them and to the right.

"I not hear anything," Dega said.

"There is something in there. I am certain."

As if to prove her correct, the thicket crackled and out ambled a black bear cub.

"God, no!" Evelyn cried, and raised her rifle.

Chapter Five

Spotted Wolf called an early halt for the day on the bank of a stream dotted by cottonwoods. The women went to gather wood.

Earlier in the day Tall Bull had dropped a doe with an arrow. Of late, their fare had consisted mainly of rabbit and other small animals, so they were looking forward to juicy deer meat.

Tall Bull, helped by Tangle Hair, did the skinning and butchering. The boy was fond of intestines and cut off a small section to chew on while they worked.

Careful to move his hair so he did not sit on it, Spotted Wolf sat cross-legged and watched everyone. His rifle was across his lap.

Twilight had about given way to night. The women got a fire going, and the splash of light held the dark at bay.

Spotted Wolf listened to the sounds of the prairie and heard nothing out of the ordinary. All was as it should be. He had been worried about the whites they encountered, but there had been no sign of them. By now, he assumed, the whites were well up in the foothills. He hoped they ran into some Blackfeet. That would teach them to be so arrogant.

The aroma of the roasting meat made Spotted Wolf's mouth water. The others were staring at the haunch on the spit, eager to eat. Tangle Hair was chewing on yet another piece of intestine.

Soon Buffalo Calf Woman announced the meat was done. Spotted Wolf ate leisurely, tearing at the succulent flesh with his strong teeth and then slowly chewing, savoring each piece. When at length he was done, he licked his fingers clean.

Tangle Hair continued to eat long after the rest of them.

Now came the favorite part of Spotted Wolf's day. Opening his parfleche, he took out his pipe and his bag of tobacco. The tobacco was his most prized possession. As a member of the Tobacco Society, this year it was his turn to lead the sacred Tobacco Ceremony. Only members of the Society planted and harvested tobacco.

Spotted Wolf filled the bowl of his pipe and prepared to smoke. As if by unspoken agreement, the rest gathered near, and Tangle Hair, as he did every night, said, "Tell us a story."

"Which story?" Spotted Wolf asked him.

"How the world was made," the boy said, his eyes aglow. "I like that one the most."

Spotted Wolf puffed on his pipe, drawing the smoke deep into his lungs. A sense of peace and contentment spread through him. "Long ago there was no land. Only water, and four ducks.

One day the maker of all that is, Old Man Coyote, came across the four ducks. 'Which of you has more courage than the rest?' he asked them.

"One little duck said that he did. Old Man Coyote told him to dive to the bottom of the water and bring up some mud. The duck dived and was gone a long time. When the duck came back up, it had mud on its beak. Old Man Coyote held the mud until it was dry, then blew on it. Land spread across the world, and since that day has shared the world with water."

"What if the duck had not reached the bottom and brought dirt back up?" Tangle Hair asked. "Would there be any land?"

"Who can say? That is a good question, though." Spotted Wolf waited, and when no one else had a comment, he went on. "The ducks requested of Old Man Coyote that he make more. 'There are just the four of us,' they said. 'Where are other livings things that we might share the land and the water with them?'

"Old Man Coyote blew on the dirt again, and the first man and woman were formed. These were the first Crows. They were naked but did not know they were naked because they were blind. Old Man Coyote opened their eyes, and the first thing they did was ask for clothes."

"I would have asked for a lance or a bow," Tangle Hair said, "so I could protect myself from my enemies."

"The Crows had no enemies then," Spotted Wolf reminded him. "There were no other people." He paused. "Next, Old Man Coyote blew on the dirt, and from it came all the plants and animals. Among them were the buffalo. Old Man Coyote showed the man and the woman how to kill a buffalo and which parts to eat and use."

"That is why there are so many of them," Tall Bull interjected. "So we will never be in want."

"The buffalo will always be," Spotted Bull agreed. "And as long as they exist so will the Crows."

"Tell us the story of the boy who could lift buffalo," Tangle Hair requested.

Spotted Wolf smiled. It was a favorite of the young. "Deep in the mountains live the Little People. They live in caves. They want nothing to do with us or any other tribe and keep to themselves. Because of this, we do not know a lot about them. Two things, though, we do know. One, they are great with the bow, and can shoot a pine cone out of a man's hand at fifty paces. The other thing that we know is that they are so strong, any one of them can pick up a buffalo and carry it on his shoulders."

"To be that strong!" Tangle Hair marveled.

"One day the Crows were on the move. As they went through the mountains, a baby fell from its travois and no one noticed. The baby was asleep. It did not wake up until the Crows were far away. It was hungry, and it began to cry, but there was no one near. Except the Little People.

"They gathered around the baby and talked about what to do. Some wanted to leave it there since it was not one of theirs. But others of the Little People said it was only a baby, and how could they leave it to die? So it was that they took the baby and raised him as one of their own. They fed it the food they ate and dressed it in the hides they wore.

"At first the child was weak and a lot of bother. But the Little People did not give up, and a change took place. The child became as they were. It became immensely strong, could run as fast as they do, and as an archer he was without equal. From time to time he came to live among the Crows for a while, but he always went back to the Little People. He would go on buffalo hunts, and to see him pick up a buffalo left everyone in awe."

"I would like to hear about his fight with the beast that would not die," Tangle Hair requested.

Spotted Wolf regarded the stars and sniffed deep of the wood smoke. "Tomorrow night. We must get an early start. We need our rest."

"I will sit up first," the boy offered.

Normally, Spotted Wolf and Tall Bull would keep watch. But since their trip had been uneventful, except for their brief run-in with the four whites, they had been letting the boy take a turn.

"Keep a sharp eye, son," Tall Bull instructed. "If you hear anything unusual, anything at all, wake us."

"I will, Father. You can depend on me."

Later, as Spotted Wolf lay with his wife's cheek on his shoulder, he caressed her hair and asked, "Are you ever sorry we did not have more children?"

Buffalo Calf Woman raised her head to look at him. "Have you been drinking the white man's firewater?"

Spotted Wolf chuckled. Among his people there was a saying: The Crow who drank firewater was no longer a Crow. "I am serious. Do you wish we had more?"

"Three was enough," Buffalo Calf Woman said, settling back down. "I almost died with the last one."

Spotted Wolf remembered and shuddered.

"Why do you ask? The boy?"

"He makes me think of how it was when ours were his age," Spotted Wolf admitted. "They were good winters."

"Yes, they were," Buffalo Calf Woman said. "But now our hair is turning gray, and there will be no more talk of more children." She paused, then raised her head again. "Unless you want to take another wife. Is that what this is about?"

Rubbing her shoulder, Spotted Wolf replied, "One woman is all I could handle. I am happy with you."

"Are you certain? I have seen how Moon Woman looks at you when she thinks you will not notice."

Spotted Wolf laughed. He did not make any noise. He simply lay there silently laughing, his entire body quaking. Moon Woman was notorious among the Crows for two traits: she hated men, and she was as big as her namesake. The idea of her being interested in him was preposterous.

"You must be sick," Buffalo Calf Woman said. "You have chills."

Spotted Wolf laughed even more. When at last his mirth subsided, he grinned at her and said, "I knew there was a reason I took you into my lodge."

"I thought it was my cooking."

"You are a fine wife. Have I ever told you that?"

"Once a day for forty winters."

"Has it been that long?" Spotted Wolf said. "Sometimes it seems like only yesterday that you caught my eye. Have you been happy with me?"

"We have had a good life, husband. Had I to live it again, I would do the same."

Spotted Wolf closed his eyes. The feel of her warm body against his, the crackle of the fire, soon lulled him into drifting off. He could not say how long he had slept, although it was quite a while, when a sound brought him out of the dream world into the world of the living. Right away he knew that something was wrong. He glanced toward the fire.

Tangle Hair was sprawled on the ground, blood trickling from a gash in his temple.

Spotted Wolf started to sit up but stopped when metal clicked and the muzzle of a rifle touched his forehead. "No you don't, chief. Stay right where you are if you know what's good for you." He looked up into the cold, flat eyes of the white man called Bodin.

The mulatto and the one with muscles stood over Tall Bull. The fourth white man stood well back where he could shoot anyone who resisted.

"I bet you're surprised to see us again, huh, chief?"

"I hoped I would not," Spotted Wolf said. Buffalo Calf Woman mumbled and stirred and went to sit up, but he held on to her, whispering in her ear, "Do not move. We are in a bad way."

Tall Bull was still asleep. The white man with muscles jabbed him in the neck with the barrel of his rifle and he sat up, glancing about in confusion while groping for his bow and quiver.

"Are these what you are looking for?" the mulatto asked, and tossed them into the dark.

"Take furs. Go," Spotted Wolf said to Bodin. "They what you want."

"How would you know?" Bodin retorted. Smirking, he took several steps back. "You are in for it now, chief, and that is no lie."

Spotted Wolf felt about for his rifle, which had been next to him. It was gone. Then he saw it, in the grass behind Bodin. "Hurt us and my people hurt you."

"That trick worked once, but it won't work again," Bodin said. "We've been watching your back trail, chief. There are just the five of you. No one else."

"When they find us dead, they hunt you."

"By then we will be so far away, they will never find us," Bodin declared. He sidled to the packs, squatted, and ran his hand over the hides. "Soft as a baby's backside. When we trade them, we'll get good value."

"Take furs. Go," Spotted Wolf repeated.

"You haven't been paying attention, chief. The hides aren't all we came for. We came for fun, too."

"Fun?" Spotted Wolf said.

Bodin nodded at the mulatto, who went over to Tangle Hair, smiled down at him, then, with lightning quickness, drew his knife and buried the blade between the boy's shoulder blades. The *thunk* was loud and ugly.

"Tangle Hair!" Tall Bull cried, and pushed to his feet, or tried to. He was only halfway up when the white with the muscles smashed the butt of his rifle against Tall Bull's head. Tall Bull collapsed, his limbs twitching. Owl Woman also tried to rise but was seized by the hair and flung onto her back.

"Where do you think you are going, squaw?" the one with the muscles demanded. "Each of us gets to take a turn with you. We drew straws, and I'm first."

"No," Spotted Wolf said softly.

"Oh, yes, Injun," Bodin gloated. "And he likes to make them scream when he does them."

Buffalo Calf Woman swept from under the blankets with her knife in her hand. She thrust at Bodin's throat, but he dodged and saved himself by the thinness of a hair. In doing so, he tripped over Spotted Wolf's rifle. She flung herself at him. Her knees came down on his stomach, whooshing the breath from his lungs. For a moment he was limp and helpless, and she raised her knife overhead to slay him.

The boom of a rifle was unnaturally loud. At the blast, the top of Buffalo Calf Woman's head exploded

Bodin was gasping for breath. He pushed her body off, swiped at the gore on his shirt, and growled, "Teak, what the hell!"

"Would you rather I let her stab you?"

"No. But you didn't have to kill her. You could have winged her. Now all we have left is the one."

"You're welcome," Teak said.

Sitting up, Bodin glared at Spotted Wolf. "That bitch of yours had sand. I'll say that for her."

His head spinning in a whirlwind of emotion,

Spotted Wolf managed to choke out. "She was fine woman."

Bodin drew a pistol and thumbed back the hammer. "Any last words, chief? We'll take your furs up into the high country with us, kill time for a month, then mosey down to Bent's Fort to trade them. By then no one will connect us with you if by some miracle someone is looking."

In his own tongue, Spotted Wolf said, "I call on Old Man Coyote for revenge. I ask that you be punished, all of you. I beg that you die, and die horribly."

"I don't know what all that prattle was about," Bodin said, "but I trust it was worth spending your final moments." He smiled and squeezed the trigger.

Chapter Six

Degamawaku drew rein in shock. Nansusequa never took life without cause. To defend themselves, or when they hunted, those were valid reasons. Even then, the Nansusequa believed that life must be taken with reverence, keeping in mind that That Which Is In All Things was also in whatever they killed. For the girl he adored to whip up her rifle and point it at a harmless cub was, to him, a breach of all he held dear. "No!" he cried.

Evelyn's skin was crawling. It always did at the sight of a bear. Ever since she was little, hardly a year went by that her family did not tangle with one. She had seen her father severely mauled, and sat by his bedside as he fought for life. It would be fine with her if all the bears in the Rockies were to keel over. The world was a safer place without them. "The mother!" she yelled back at Dega. "Where is the mother?"

That was the danger. Normally, black bears avoided humans. But a mother bear with young cubs was not normal. Her maternal instinct was aroused, and it did not take much to send her into a towering rage.

The cub stopped and looked at them and uttered a low cry.

"Scat!" Evelyn shouted, waving an arm. "Shoo!"

But the cub did not move. It stared at them, evidently curious.

"We will swing around," Evelyn proposed. "If the mother comes after us I'll try to bring her down." It would not be easy. Bears were notoriously tough to kill. In addition to thick layers of muscle and fat that protected their vitals, their skulls were exceptionally thick. Thick enough to deflect a lead slug.

Dega was worried the mother bear would appear. He wanted to get out of there as quickly as possible to forestall the taking of life. Kneeing his horse past Evelyn's, he reined to the left to put more distance between them and the cub.

Evelyn followed. She got a crick in her neck from gazing back for so long. Eventually, though, they were in among pines, and safe. The cub had stayed by the thicket. "That was a close one," she remarked.

Dega had never thought to ask her how she felt about killing. He had taken it for granted she felt as he did, but now it dawned on him that she was not Nansusequa. She was, in fact, half white and half red. Granted, she had more of her father in her than her mother; that was plain from her face and her hair and her eyes. But she was still what most called a halfbreed, and it was said that half-breeds had violent natures. Clearing his throat, he asked, "You kill many things?"

"What kind of question is that?" Evelyn asked. "If the mother bear had come after us, I wouldn't have had any choice."

"We ride from her," Dega said.

Evelyn rested her Hawken across her saddle. "You haven't owned that horse long. And if I remember right, your people back east did not have horses, did they?"

"No," Dega confirmed.

"Then there is something you should know. Bears might be big and heavy. They might look to be as slow as turtles. But they're not. Over short distances, some bears can overtake a horse."

"You say bears catch horses?"

"They can, yes. If I have to decide between outriding a bear and shooting it, I'll shoot the monster."

This was a revelation to Dega, and deeply troubling. To take his mind off it, he asked, "What be monster?"

"A monster is a scary creature, like a bear," Evelyn explained. "One of my pa's books tells the story of a man who makes one from the parts of dead people."

Dega glanced at her to see if it was some sort of joke. Now and again her humor eluded him. "Dead people?"

"Yes. The book is called *Frankenstein, or, the Modern Prometheus.* It was written by a girl slightly older than I am."

"Dead people?" Dega said again.

"Victor Frankenstein takes a bunch of body parts and sews them together and reanimates the whole thing."

Dega absorbed that. He considered her words every way he could think of, and it still led to the same conclusion. "Whites can do that?"

Evelyn laughed merrily. "Goodness gracious, no. It's a story. Make-believe. Fiction, we call it. When you learn to read you can read it for yourself, but be warned, it can scare the socks off you."

Dega tried to remember what socks were. "You like read story?"

"I sure did. I can't think of any book that scared me more."

"You like be scared?"

"So long as it's a book and not real life," Evelyn said. "It's a lot more fun to read about a monster ripping throats out than to have a bear try to rip out yours."

"That fun?" Dega could not imagine how. Throat-ripping was throat-ripping, no matter how you looked at it.

"Sure is," Evelyn said. "To tell you the truth, I have been wondering if maybe I should try my hand at writing. I think it is something I would like. Something I would like very much."

"You make book?"

"I might write one, yes. Getting it published is another matter. I would not know how to go about it."

Dega glanced back. "What you write?"

Evelyn shifted in her saddle and encompassed the valley with a sweep of her arm. "I would write about this. About life in the wild. You have to admit, I know more about it than most since I've lived in the wilderness all my life."

"Other whites read book?"

"I would hope so. Most live east of the Mississippi River and have no notion of what the frontier is like."

Memories of his family's perilous crossing of that broad, turbulent waterway on their journey west washed over Dega.

"Let's pick up the pace," Evelyn suggested. "I'm still not convinced we are safe from that mother bear."

The sun continued on its golden arc as they climbed. The rocky crags that once seemed so impossibly high above them were near enough now that a few stunted trees and snippets of vegetations could be discerned.

Evelyn let herself relax. She breathed deep of the invigorating mountain air and reveled in the view and the beauty around her. She did not get up this far very often. Miles off to the west glistened the pale sheen of the glacier that fed the lake. Her brother and his wife had gone up for a closer look at the glacier a while ago and nearly paid for their curiosity with their lives.

Her gaze drifted to Degamawaku. She admired his handsome profile when he turned his head. She admired, too, how he sat his horse. He had a natural ease about him that she found appealing. The notion bore home the fact that she'd become quite fond of him. He was the best friend she ever had.

They skirted a talus slope and came to a barren

bench. From here they could see clear to the far end of the valley. The lake was a blue jewel in the center of green velvet. The cabins were smaller than thimbles.

"Here will do us," Evelyn said, and drew rein.

Dega regarded the high ramparts still a goodly distance off. "We see mountain sheep?"

"That we will." Grinning, Evelyn swung down. She stretched, then opened a parfleche and rummaged inside.

Dega stiffly dismounted. He was not accustomed to spending half a day on horseback. His lower back was particularly sore, and he arched it to relieve a cramp. He turned as Evelyn took a metal cylinder from the parfleche.

"Ever seen one of these?"

"No."

"You are in for a treat. It's called a spyglass." Evelyn beckoned and moved along the bench about fifty yards to where they had a clear view of the cliffs. Leaning her rifle against her leg to free her hands, she extended the telescope to its full length and put the eyepiece to her eye. A slight adjustment and the cliffs were brought so near, she felt as if she could reach out and touch them. Grinning in anticipation of Dega's reaction, she held the spyglass out to him. "Have a look-see."

Dega did as she had done. At first he saw nothing. Then, with startling clarity, he was looking at a crack in a rock wall from which jutted several blades of grass. He lowered the spyglass, raised it to his eye, then lowered it again. "Where?" he asked uncertainly.

Evelyn pointed at the cliffs. "It brings things that are far off up close."

Dega aligned the spyglass with a patch of white on the summit. The patch became snow. He told her what he saw.

"Even in the summer, snow falls that high up. But it won't last long. It's not like in the winter when the snow up here is twelve feet deep. Here, let me look again."

Evelyn took the telescope and scanned the cliff face for half a mile in both directions. Soon her patience was rewarded. "So you have never seen a mountain sheep? Well, there's one." Holding the telescope steady, she moved aside. "Take a gander."

Dega put his eye to the spyglass. The animal he beheld was standing on a rocky point above a precipice, its head erect, its large horns curling around its ears. He saw it blink, saw its nostrils flare. "I want reach out to touch it"

"You would think you could say boo and make it jump," Evelyn said.

Boo was a new one to Dega. But he worked out that she meant they could scare it.

"You can borrow the spyglass any time you want, you know," Evelyn mentioned. "Show it to your family."

Dega pulled back and accidentally brushed her arm. The contact, though fleeting, sent a tingle through him, clear down to his toes. His mouth went suddenly dry, and he quickly looked away so she would not notice his discomfort.

"We will eat the food I packed, then head down in an hour or so. Unless you have an objection."

"Sorry?" Dega's head was in an odd sort of whirl.

"If it's all right with you."

"Yes. All right."

They walked toward the horses, Evelyn chatting about the fine weather and the view and wasn't it wonderful their families had the valley all to themselves. Dega barely heard her. His lightheadedness persisted, until, by force of will and a shake of his head, he cleared it.

"—have a cabin of my own, I wouldn't want it on the lake," Evelyn was telling him. "It is downright crowded. No, I want my cabin along one of the streams that feed into the lake. The stream farthest south, say. What do you think?"

"Think fine."

"You do? I have a spot picked out. Maybe you have seen it? Where a meadow runs along one side of the stream? Plenty of graze for livestock. And that meadow is downright gorgeous in the spring and summer, what with all the wildflowers."

Although she could not say why, Evelyn had been to the site half a dozen times in recent weeks. She would go and sit on the bank with her feet dangling in the water, and imagine a cabin and a corral and how peaceful life there would be. Which was ironic, she reflected, because at one time she had been dead set on living anywhere *but* the mountains. She had hated frontier life, hated the dangers and the uncertainties. To her way of thinking, civilization had been better. Civilization, where a person could walk out their door without fear of running into a grizzly or a painter. Civilization, where there were no hostiles out to count coup and renegade whites were held in check by minions of the law.

Then came her kidnapping, and Evelyn had learned a painful truth. Civilization had dangers of its own, dangers every bit as deadly as a grizzly or a mountain lion.

When it came right down to it, Evelyn had discovered, the main difference between life on the frontier and so-called civilized life was that on the frontier the dangers did not hide behind a friendly smile or a lecherous eye.

"The horses," Dega abruptly said.

Evelyn glanced up. She had been so deep in thought, she had not been paying attention. "What was that?"

"The horses. They dance."

Evelyn looked. The two mounts had their ears pricked and were staring at the ground and prancing. She broke into a run, struck by a premonition.

"Something wrong?" Dega asked, matching her stride.

"Could be," Evelyn said, flying now. She was upset with herself for not using picket pins. If her father had warned her once about leaving a horse untended, he had warned her a thousand times. Yet still she forgot.

The dun whinnied in fright. Her buttermilk reared.

"No, no, no," Evelyn said, exerting herself to her utmost. A faint sound reached her, reminiscent of dry seeds in a gourd. A rattling sound as distinct as the screech of a mountain lion or the howl of a wolf. Only one creature in all existence made that sound.

Dega heard, too. He had been puzzled by the antics of their animals and Evelyn's urgency, but now he understood. He pulled ahead of her, afraid his dun would be bitten. Suddenly, to his consternation, the dun wheeled and raced toward the end of the bench. He shouted to it to stop in Nansusequa, but it paid him no heed.

Evelyn was afraid her buttermilk would do the same, leaving them stranded afoot. She saw that both horses had drifted to an area littered with rocks. The perfect place for rattlesnakes to lie in the sun and warm themselves.

The dun disappeared over the rim.

Dega kept running. He could not catch his mount, but he could help Evelyn get hers.

Suddenly the buttermilk reared a second time. When its front hooves came down, the rattling ceased.

With a lunge, Dega snagged the bridle. He turned toward Evelyn just as she ran up.

"Thank you. I'll go catch your horse." Evelyn reached for the reins, then froze. Directly in front of her a sinuous form had risen up out of the rocks.

The rattling resumed, only louder, as the rattlesnake bared its venomous fangs.

Chapter Seven

Nate King was trying, for the fourth time, to impale a worm on the bone hook at the end of his fishing line when he heard someone approach. He did not need to look up to know who it was. A throaty chuckle told him.

"How now, Horatio? I see you are wrestling a worm and the worm is winning."

"These critters are too blamed slippery," Nate complained. He had dug a handful of worms out of the ground half an hour ago. Two had been taken by fish that pulled free of the hook.

Shakespeare McNair hunkered and regarded the worm with amusement. Like Nate, he wore buckskins. Like Nate, he had a powder horn, ammo pouch and possibles bag crisscrossed across his chest. Similarly, he was armed with a brace of pistols and a knife, but not a bowie like Nate's. They both had beards, but where Nate's was black, Shakespeare's beard and hair were as white as snow. "My money is on the worm."

"Don't you have someone else to bother?"

"Not at the moment, no." Shakespeare settled back, placed his Hawken beside him, and gazed out over the placid blue of the lake. "Nice day for fishing if you know how to fish."

Nate sighed. "I would kick you, but I might drop the worm."

"It might be best if you did." /

"You would use another?" Nate said while jabbing the hook at the worm and sticking it in his own finger.

"How prove ye that in the great heap of your knowledge?" McNair said, quoting his namesake. "I would use that one, but I would drop it in the dirt first and let it roll around some."

"What good would that do?"

"The dirt sticks to the worm and makes the worm easier to hold, and easier to thread onto a hook."

Nate tried it. He rolled the worm back and forth using a fingertip. When the worm was good and covered with bits of dirt, he picked it up again and found it simple to impale. "Dang you."

"Excuse me?" Shakespeare rejoined. "I offer sage advice and you castigate me? Would the fountain of your mind were clear again, that I might water an ass at it."

"Spare me the bard for a moment and explain something," Nate said. "How is it that in all the years I have known you, you never saw fit to mention that trick?"

"I had no idea you were so godawful at hooking worms or I would have," Shakespeare answered. "It is embarrassing to have a friend who is so puny."

Nate flicked the line out over the water and watched the worm sink from sight. "For some reason Winona wants fish tonight. She hardly ever wants fish."

"Given how much trouble that worm was giving you," Shakespeare said, "it is a good thing your wife is not hungry for chipmunk."

"Enough about the worm."

"A serviceable villain, as duteous to the vices of thy mistress as badness would desire," Shakespeare quoted. "But very well. Let us have enough of worms and talk about more important matters." He opened his possibles bag and removed a silver flask. "Care for a nip?"

Nate was surprised. "Since when did you take to drinking in the middle of the day?"

"I detect an accusation," McNair replied good-naturedly. "But as the bard himself put it, drink is a great provider of three important things."

"What might they be?"

"Nose-painting, sleep and urine. When you get my age, you never get enough of the second and have way too much of the third."

"And the nose-paint?"

Shakespeare started to tip the flask to his lips. "What is a red nose between friends?" He took a nice long swig, exhaled in contentment, and again held it out. "Brandy, Horatio. I bought some the last time I was at Bent's. It has a medicinal effect on aching joints."

Nate accept the flask and treated himself to a

swallow. It had been so long since he had spirits of any kind, he had a fit of coughing.

"My word. First you can't handle a worm and now you can't handle your liquor. It must be the worry."

Nate concentrated on the line. "What do I have to worry about?"

"I saw your youngest and her green Galahad go riding off up the mountain this morning," Shakespeare mentioned.

"So? I trust Degamawaku. He has shown himself to be a fine young man."

"Noticed that, did you? Because the fruit of your loins certainly has. I dare say she regards him as the finest young man who ever drew breath. Her Juliet to his Romeo, as it were."

The breeze off the lake stirred Nate's long hair. A pair of ducks, male and female, winged in over the water and alighted. He scowled. "You are getting ahead of yourself. They are friends. Nothing more, nothing less."

"Less than friendship is not the issue," Shakespeare countered. "It is the more that concerns us. Some in this valley predict that before the year is out you will acquire a son-in-law."

Nate snorted. "Some? As in a certain rascal who goes around quoting William Shakespeare because he can't think of words of his own to use?"

About to take another swig, McNair colored red and sat up. "Base villain! Thou art not honest. Thy food is such as has been belched out by infected lungs."

"How did food get into this?"

"But peace, good fop," Shakespeare said. "I won't hold it against you. I would feel the same if I were in your moccasins."

"I have no idea what you are talking about." Nate thought he saw the line move and tensed to pull on the pole.

"Fibber. The subject is daughters in love and the young men who love them."

"Cut it out. There has been no talk of love by either. They say they are friends and only friends."

"And you believe them, ticklebrain?"

"Let's just say I don't think either of them have any interest in taking it any further at this time," Nate replied. "If love is on the horizon, so be it, but I will jump that hurdle when it crops up in front of me."

"Ah." Shakespeare tilted the flask, then smacked his lips. "I keep forgetting that a large part of parenthood is denial."

Nate thought the line jiggled. He almost jerked it but decided to wait. "Look. I admit Evelyn is growing up. She is a young woman now, not a little girl. But that does not mean she is ready to take a husband. It could be years yet before she reaches that point."

Shakespeare held the flask out again, but Nate shook his head. "Very well. If you insist that the boulder about to fall on your head is really a feather, as your best friend and mentor, I will play along with your delusion."

The line jumped, and the pole was nearly pulled from Nate's grasp. Firming his hold, he played the fish, seeking to tire it out as he brought it closer to shore. "I've hooked a big one!"

"Careful! Don't give it too much slack," Shakespeare cautioned.

Nate was doing his best to keep the line tight, but the frantic fish was streaking in all different directions. He whipped the pole back and immediately wished he hadn't; the line stopped moving. He quickly brought the hook in, only to find the worm gone.

Shakespeare McNair chortled. "Maybe you should ask your wife if she wouldn't rather have chipmunk, after all."

Evelyn King had no time to react. The rattlesnake struck as she set eyes on it. She tried to spring aside, but her reflexes were not the equal of the serpent's. The rattlesnake bit her.

Evelyn went to scream in terror, then realized the snake had bitten her dress, not her leg. She spun to one side, expecting the rattler to go flying, but instead its body flailed the air in a frenzy. She whipped the other way, with the same result. Only then did she perceive what had happened; its fangs were caught in her dress and would not come loose.

Degamawaku's chest seemed to explode when the rattlesnake struck. Of all the creatures in the forest, he found it hardest to think fondly of snakes. That Which Is In All Things was also supposed to be in them, but that did not heighten his fondness any. Nor did the death of a kindly Nansusequa woman, bitten while strolling through the woods with her children.

Now he saw the rattler's fangs sink into Evelyn and he opened his mouth to cry out, but his vocal cords would not work. He saw her spin, saw the snake thrash, and heard her yell, "It can't let go!"

Dega found his voice. "Stand still!"

"No!" Evelyn was afraid that if she did, the rattler would continue to flail about and its fangs would pierce her leg.

"Please!" Dega urged. He reached out to stop her but then stopped himself, afraid he might cause her to trip, with dire consequences. "Stand still! I have idea. Trust me!"

Evelyn slowed in her mad spinning. Either the rattler was tiring or it was dizzy—if snakes could even get dizzy—because it was not struggling as fiercely. She glanced at Dega and was deeply touched by the concern on his handsome face. Reluctantly, against her better judgment, she stood perfectly still except for the heaving of her bosom. The rattler hung limp at her side. "Whatever you plan to do," she said between gasps for breath, "you had better do it quick."

Dega dropped to his knees. The snake's tail still buzzed, but otherwise it was not moving. Until that moment he had not appreciated how big it was. Fully as long as his arm, and as thick around as his wrist, its scales glistened in the sunlight. Its eyes, so different from the eyes of other living things, had that intense baleful glare that had unnerved him as a youth. His skin crawling, Dega slowly reached up and gripped the snake behind its head.

Instantly, the rattler went into another frenzy. It twisted and tried to coil, the lower half of its body repeatedly hitting Dega. He held on until the snake quieted save for the buzzing of the rattles.

Sweat caked him, including his palms, and he hoped he would not lose his grip.

Evelyn did not move a muscle. She was braced for the sharp sting of the reptile's fangs, but so far she had been spared. "Maybe take my knife and cut the head off," she suggested.

"Kill only when must," Dega said. "That Nansusequa way."

"Which is fine and dandy," Evelyn told him. "But I am the one standing here with a snake stuck on my dress."

Dega leaned closer. He focused on the fangs and tried to ignore how close he was to Evelyn. Another bout of lightheadedness now might prove harmful to both of them. He slowly turned the snake's blunt triangular head from side to side, and the cloth its fangs were hooked to moved in the corresponding direction. "It very stuck."

"The trick is to *unstick* it," Evelyn said with more irritation than she intended. "And the easiest way to do that is cut off the head."

"Please," Dega said. He had never imagined she could be so violent. Among his people, those who habitually harbored violent thoughts were believed to have lost that special inner sense of That Which Is In All Things.

"All right. But this is not doing my nerves any good." Evelyn was miffed that he seemed to consider saving the rattler more important than the risk to her life.

Dega pulled the snake back as far as the dress permitted. The fangs did not give way. He twisted to the right, then twisted to the left, but they were still caught fast. Then inspiration came to him. "I have idea."

"I hope it is a good one."

"It very good," Dega said, certain she would like it. "I cut dress."

"What?"

"I cut hole in dress. Unstick you and snake. Snake be fine. You be fine." Dega beamed.

"My dress won't be fine," Evelyn said in considerable annoyance. "It took me over a week to make, too. I would rather not have a hole in it, thank you very much."

"But we save snake." Dega did not understand why she was against it. When given a choice between taking life and sparing it, the People of the Forest always chose the former.

"If you say that one more time I will scream," Evelyn said.

Her comment caused Dega great worry. She must be extremely upset, he reasoned. Somehow he had hurt her feelings. He tried to think of what he could say that would soothe her, but he just did not know enough white words. "I sorry you mad."

"I'm not mad," Evelyn responded, although if she wasn't, it was a close thing. "I just want to be shed of my new appendage."

"That why cut dress."

"Is there no other way?"

"I not think of one," Dega admitted. He wished he could. He sought to soothe her by stressing, "It just dress."

"You did hear me say I made it? And that it took over a week? Yet you still want to cut it?"

The disappointment in her voice caused Dega to shrivel inside. "I hear you."

"Then go ahead."

Working swiftly, Dega cut a square around the rattlesnake's head. The moment he separated the rattler and the square from the dress, he placed the snake on the ground and his right foot on top of it behind the head, pinning it so it could not bite him as he gingerly pried the fabric from its fangs with the tip of the knife blade.

With a parting angry hiss, the serpent slithered off into the rocks.

"You safe now," Dega said proudly.

Evelyn went to thank him, and stiffened. They had been so preoccupied with the rattler that they had forgotten about her horse.

It, too, was gone.

Chapter Eight

Ranks of lodgepole pines rose tall and somber on all sides. In places the boles were so close together that Evelyn brushed her shoulders against them. Not much sunlight penetrated, with the result that the forest floor was shrouded in perpetual shadow. As a little girl she always thought lodgepole woods were spooky, and she had not changed her opinion.

Evelyn held her Hawken level at her waist, thankful she had her weapons. That was her one consolation in this whole mess. Without weapons they would be a lot worse off.

Evelyn remembered her father reading to her from a book once. She couldn't recollect the name of the writer, but he had gone on about how the wilderness was paradise, and about how the ideal state of the world, as he called it, was for all things to be as natural. She particularly recalled a page where he gushed on about walking as one with the animals and at peace with all creation.

He wrote a scene where bears and deer and squirrels and snakes and everything else intermingled in peaceful rapture.

The man was an idiot.

The wilderness was not anything like that. Meat-eaters and plant-eaters did not walk paw-in-hoof through cathedral forests, smiling fang and tooth at one another.

In the real world, in the wilderness Evelyn knew, the meat-eaters ate the plant-eaters. Mountain lions did not frolic with bucks and does. Roving wolves that came on fawns lying in the high grass did not give them an affectionate lick. Bears were not friends with fish. In the real world, meat-eaters were always on the lookout to pounce on the unwary and rip them with claw and fang.

The notion that all things could get along as if they were brothers and sisters was ridiculous. Animals killed other animals to survive. From the biggest to the littlest, they killed. Birds ate bugs and worms and were in turn eaten by snakes and bobcats and the like. Everything from chipmunks on up to elk were food for something else. There was no brotherly love among the creatures of the woodland and the prairie.

The natural state was not heaven. The natural state was kill or be killed.

Evelyn had learned that bitter lesson almost before she could walk. The wilds were filled with peril, and death awaited those who ignored the dangers. She had hated that fact. For years it had colored her outlook toward the wilderness, and been a factor in her early preference for civilization over the wild.

It never struck her as fair or right that her life had to constantly be in danger. What sort of existence was that? To be born only to live in constant fear of becoming dead? To her it had seemed too stupid for words.

Only later in life did it occur to her that there was a certain fairness in that the law of survival applied to all creatures, not just her. It was not as if she had been singled out. All living things, every moment they were alive, lived under the hovering blade of the guillotine of death.

It still made no sense, but that was life.

Human beings, however, had found out how to buck the odds. They found a way to delay the descent of the guillotine. They had developed weapons.

Evelyn would be the first to admit that without her rifle and pistols and knife, she would be as helpless as a baby bird or that fawn in the high grass. Her weapons enabled her to stay alive. Only her weapons could keep the predators at bay.

"What you thinking?" Dega unexpectedly asked.

The question so startled her that Evelyn nearly jumped. She glanced over her shoulder. He looked as downcast as she had ever seen him. "Sorry. I do that a lot. Some people say I think too much."

Degamawaku did not understand why she apologized. Among the Nansusequa thinking was encouraged. It was by the harmony of thought that life was kept in balance. "You still mad at horses?"

Evelyn grew prickly just thinking about them.

"I sure as blazes am. They know not to do that, but they did it anyway."

"How know?" Dega asked.

"My pa brought them up, broke them to saddle, trained them. He spends hours breaking them of their skittishness."

Thankful she was talking again, Dega prompted her with, "How he do that?"

"Oh, there are various ways. He will shake a blanket near their legs, or fire a gun near them so they get used to the sound, or he will shake an old rattler tail he has."

"That make horses brave?"

Evelyn's mouth curled in a smile. "All except the rattler's tail seem to do some good. Horses never shake their fear of snakes no matter how hard he tries."

"Then why be mad?" Dega inquired. He hoped he was not overstepping himself. Whites were so different from the People of the Forest that he did not know what was permissible to say.

Evelyn laughed. "I am more mad at me than I am at them," she confessed. "It was my fault they ran off. If I had tied them like my pa always keeps reminding me to do, we wouldn't be following them right now, we would be riding them."

"You blame you?" This was an insight Dega had not foreseen.

"Who else would I blame? You can't blame a horse for being a horse. If it sounded like I did, I was only complaining to hear myself talk."

Dega laboriously pieced together her meaning. "You say mean words about horses to hear yourself say mean words?"

"Pretty much, yes."

"Ah." Dega sought the logic in that, but it eluded him.

"Don't you like to let off steam when you are mad?"

"Sorry? What is steam?" Dega was proud of himself for using *is* instead of *be*.

"That was a figure of speech," Evelyn said with her gaze glued to the forest floor and the hoof-prints she was tracking. "It means to air your lungs. To get all the anger out of your system by letting it loose on the wind."

"There anger in you?"

Something in his tone made Evelyn look at him. "Everyone has anger in them at one time or another. Everyone gets mad."

Degamawaku admired a shaft of sunlight that had pierced the canopy, glittering with dust motes. "Nansusequa teach anger bad. Teach get mad bad."

"So what are you saying? That you never get mad or angry? That is not true and you know it. You told me yourself how mad you were when you saw your village attacked. You said you were so mad, you wanted to kill every white there." Shaking her head, Evelyn said, "Don't pretend to be something you are not and never can be. We all have feelings and they will not be denied."

Images of the slaughter of his people filtered through Dega's memory. He felt, once again, the hurt and the sickness and, yes, the fury that had coursed through his veins. "You think not get mad be wrong?"

"There is no right or wrong to being mad. It

just happens," Evelyn said. "It is like breathing. You do it without thinking about it."

Dega did not agree. "To be mad not right," he firmly declared.

"Well then, I sure am wrong a lot," Evelyn said, and laughed. "My brother is to blame for most of it, but I reckon I do have the King temper."

"Your brother Zach?"

"I only have the one, and he is more than enough. His blamed teasing has made me mad more times than there are stars in the night sky. I try not to let him get my goat, but what can you do? Brothers and sisters spat a lot. It comes naturally."

"You have goat?"

Evelyn's merriment tinkled to the tops of the lodgepoles. "Land sakes, no. That was another expression. When we say someone is getting our goat, it means they make us angry."

Dega began to despair of ever speaking her language. According to his father, the white tongue had more words than that of the Nansuse-qua. And as he was discovering first hand, many of those words had more than one meaning. Then there were the strange combinations in which whites used them. It was all so bewildering. He mentioned that.

"I suppose the white tongue is a mouthful. But so is Shoshone and your own language. I try my best, but I get them wrong all the time."

"Do you mind brother get your goat?" Dega wondered.

"I mind being compared to the hind end of a cow. Or being told my breath smells like horse urine."

Dega could not believe what he was hearing. "Your brother *do* that?"

"And worse. He is a fiend incarnate," Evelyn said affectionately, "and he's so much older than me. But that's all right. I've held my own. When he got me really mad, I would run to my ma and pretend to cry and say he had pulled my hair. He would be in hot water for a week." She chuckled. "Those were the days."

"You say mean things at him?"

"Of course. Why do you sound so shocked? You and your sisters must have done your share of teasing."

"Not like you do," Dega said. He loved Tenikawaku and Mikikawaku too much to ever deliberately hurt them, not even with words.

Evelyn was beginning to sense a gulf between them. His upbringing and hers were so different. "Tell me something. Did you and your sisters play when you were little?"

"Play how?"

"You know. Tag. Hide and seek." Evelyn saw his confusion so she elaborated. "Chase each other, hide from each other, those sorts of things."

"Yes," Dega said, smiling, glad they had found something in common. "We play find stick, and spin-around, and we play frog." He imitated the leaping motion. "Jump over each other."

"Then you did do some normal stuff," Evelyn said, and was about to go on when a sound caused her to raise a hand for silence. It had come from up ahead.

Dega listened and heard what she had heard; a loud series of thuds. "What that be?" he whispered.

"A hoof. Come on." Evelyn made off rapidly through the lodgepoles. She had gone only a few dozen feet when the phalanx of boles gave way to scattered spruce, and there, its reins entangled in a low limb, was her buttermilk. Squealing in delight, she ran over and threw her arms around its neck. "I am so glad to see you, I can almost forgive you for running off!"

"How it get caught?" Degamawaku wanted to know.

"Beats me," Evelyn responded with a shrug. She commenced unraveling the reins. "Maybe it was scratching itself. Maybe the reins snagged as it was walking past. The good news is we have one of our animals, and we can use it to catch the other."

"Other run fast," Dega reminded her.

"Not fast enough to get way from Buttercup." Evelyn climbed on and adjusted her dress, then smiled down at him. "What are you waiting for? Swing up behind me."

Dega placed a hand on her mount's flank. "I thought you say this buttermilk."

"It is."

"But you call Butter*cup*." Try as he might, Dega could not comprehend why someone would name a horse after a cup of butter.

"Buttermilk is what whites call horses this color. Buttercup is the name I gave her. I was going to name her Bluebird because they are my favorite birds, but then I figured I should give a horse a horse name."

"Whites be strange."

"Hey, now. You are starting to sound like my brother," Evelyn playfully bantered.

Dega was shocked. "I am much sorry."

"What for, silly? I love my brother very much." Evelyn felt herself grow warm again, but this time not with anger. She beckoned. "Hop up. We're wasting daylight." It had occurred to her that if they did not catch the dun soon, they would not make it home until well after dark, and riding at night was fraught with all sorts of dangers. She extended an arm. "Grab hold."

"Very well." Dega let her help him and settled himself behind her, his lance between them.

"You might want to hold on to something," Evelyn advised. "Put a hand on my shoulder if you want." And with that, she clucked to the buttermilk and slapped her legs against its sides.

It helped that in its flight the buttermilk had been following the dun. Broken brush and freshly churned clods of dirt marked the way. Evelyn assumed the dun was bound for the valley floor and for a while it appeared to be doing so, but then it inexplicably turned to the northeast. Slowing, she reined after it. "What is this lunkhead doing?"

"Sorry?"

"Your horse is heading for the high cliffs," Evelyn explained. Only farther east than before. She noticed a lot of other tracks, those of deer and elk primarily, and it hit her that the dun was following a game trail.

"What is lunkhead?"

"Anyone or anything with less brains than

God gave a tree stump," Evelyn clarified while bent forward so she could read the sign.

"Trees have brains?" Dega distinctly recalled her saying once that the brain was what the Nansusequa called a *mota*. People had a mota, and animals had a mota, and birds had a mota, but plants most definitely did not.

"Of course not, silly goose. That's the whole point."

Now she was calling him a goose. Dega bowed his head and sighed. His desire to learn the white tongue seemed more hopeless every day. Why did it have to be so complicated?

"What in the world?"

Dega looked up. They had emerged from the trees and were climbing a bare slope. Ahead reared a high cliff. The tracks they were following clearly led right up to it—and ended. "Where horse go?"

"Your guess is as good as mine," Evelyn replied. "But it sure looks to me as if it vanished into thin air."

Chapter Nine

Evelyn King reined up. She looked to the right, she looked to the left, but there was no mistake. The horse's tracks ended at the base of the cliff.

"How that be?" Degamawaku asked.

"We're about to find out," Evelyn answered, and gigged the buttermilk. As they climbed, she had her second premonition of the day. This one filled her with mild excitement, for if she was right, it was news her father would very much want to hear. He had been saying all along that there had to be more than one way in and out of the valley. Sure enough, not long ago they had found a second, and he had used a keg of black powder to close it. As he told her afterward, "The more ways in and out there are, the more ways our enemies can get at us. It is the ones we don't know about that can do us harm. A war party could be in among us before we suspected they were here."

They were encouraged to always be on the lookout for more.

Now this.

Evelyn was less than fifteen feet from the cliff when the truth became apparent.

It was not a solid wall. There was an opening. The reason it could not be seen from below was simple: one side extended a few yards farther and overlapped the other.

Dega smiled when he saw the explanation. Nature had many wonderful tricks.

Evelyn drew rein again. She had expected a fissure, maybe, with barely enough room for a horse—or an elk. But the gap was wide enough to drive a wagon through and carpeted with grass. "Well, I'll be. We have found a secret pass."

"What we do?"

"What do you think?" Evelyn rejoined. "Where that ornery critter of yours went, we go too." She kneed Buttercup.

The walls rose high on either side, the tops seeming to reach to the clouds. The wind was louder, amplified, Evelyn guessed, by passing through what was in effect a roofless tunnel. Tracks showed that wildlife used the pass regularly. Some of the prints were of mountain buffalo. She hoped they didn't run into any. The temperamental brutes might charge on sight, and in the narrow confines of the pass, escaping would prove a challenge.

Dega was quite content to do whatever Evelyn wanted. He was not upset about the loss of the dun to the extent she was. He trusted in That Which Was In All Things, and knew that what would be, would be. If they were meant to find the dun, they would. If they were not meant to find the dun, they would not. Why be upset about something you had no control over?

The ground gently sloped downward. Twists and turns were common. Evelyn could seldom see more than fifty to sixty feet ahead. It was a long way to the bottom. When, at weary last, they emerged from a split cliff over a mile below where they had entered, it was to find the sun high in the afternoon sky.

Evelyn squinted, and frowned. There was no chance of making it home by dark now. Her folks would be worried, but it could not be helped. They would understand about the horse. Recovering it was the important thing. Horses were too valuable to simply let them run off.

Still, she hoped they might find it relatively soon. She reasoned that by the time it reached the bottom, it had been tired and hungry and thirsty. It would look for a stream, and grass.

The forest was a mix of trees, the undergrowth thick. Pine needles muffled the buttermilk's hoof falls.

Evelyn enjoyed the sun on her face, and the singing of the birds. She also liked riding double. "How are you holding up back there?"

Dega wondered what she meant. All they had done was ride through a pass. "Me fine." He caught himself and quickly amended, "Sorry. I am fine."

"Your English is getting better by the day."

Pride filled Dega. "Thank you." He almost said, *I do it for you.* But he did not.

"I think you speak it better than your pa by

now," Evelyn mentioned. When the family first arrived, only Wakumassee spoke any English.

"Maybe so," Dega conceded. But he had more incentive than his father to learn it.

"Wait until my pa hears about the pass," Evelyn said to keep the conversation going. "We'll have to ride up to watch the fireworks when he blows it up."

"Sorry?"

"My pa and Uncle Shakespeare will set a charge of black powder and bring those walls crashing down. It should be quite a sight."

"But why do that?"

"So our enemies can't get at us, silly. Pa will close every pass we find except the main one. It is better that way."

Dega thought of the tracks and what they signified. "Animals use pass. Many animals."

"They won't anymore."

"What animals do then? How they go from high on mountain to low on mountain?"

"That is for them to figure out," Evelyn said. "Maybe they won't be able to. Maybe those in our valley when the pass blows will stay there, and those down here will be stuck down here."

Dega tried to find the right words to express that it was wrong, that they were interfering with the natural order. But before he could, she leaned forward, studying the ground intently.

"Will you look at this."

"What?"

"That stupid dun isn't showing any signs of stopping. He is hurrying along as fast as his tired little hoofs will take him. And he keeps heading east. I don't know as how I like that."

"Why?"

"He should be wandering aimlessly. But he is acting like a horse with a purpose, almost as if he has a place he wants to be."

"Maybe horse does."

"Oh really?" Evelyn responded, and laughed. "Where, pray tell?" She gestured at the limitless expanse of woodland that rolled for unending miles in all directions. "We're in the middle of the Rocky Mountains. There is nothing here but wilderness and more wilderness. To him, one spot should be as good as the next."

"You know horses better," Dega said, to indicate perhaps there was something he was missing.

"That I do," Evelyn agreed. "Which is why I don't know as how I like what yours is up to."

For another hour they rode in silence save for the sounds of life around them. A squirrel chattered at them from the safety of a high branch. A doe bolted in panic. A tall-eared rabbit loped off in long bounds.

The tracks continued to lead east. Evelyn bent to examine them for the umpteenth time, as if by doing so she could solve the mystery. "East," she said aloud. "Always to the east. What is east of us? Nothing but more mountains until you come to the prairie." A sudden thought jarred her, and she snapped upright. "I'll be switched. I have figured it out."

"You have?" Dega said.

"It is a long shot but it is the only answer I can

think of. Your horse could be on its way Bent's Fort."

Dega's family had been to the trading post but once. Nate King had introduced them to one of the owners, a man named Ceran St. Vrain, and over his father's protests Nate bought them supplies and various other items the Kings and McNairs felt they needed. "Bent's Fort long way."

"That it is," Evelyn said. "But it's where my pa got that dun to begin with. He bought it from some freighters bound for Santa Fe. I bet the dun is so lost and confused, the trading post is the only place he can think of to go."

"Horse smart," Dega noted.

"For a horse it is showing an uncommon amount of sense, yes," Evelyn said. "But it is also a headache for us, because now it will be twice as hard to catch up to him. We might not get home for days."

Dega imagined spending several nights with her and grew so uncomfortably warm, he broke out in a sweat.

"My folks will have a fit. So will yours, I reckon. But we have to do it," Evelyn went on. "By morning pa will be after us. Uncle Shakespeare and Zach maybe, too. As fast as they can cover ground, it would not surprise me if they catch up to us before we are halfway to Bent's." She paused. "Let's see. It's a ten-day ride. That means we can expect to see them in four or five days, maybe less depending on how worried they are, and pa is liable to be worried something fearsome."

"Why worry them? Why not go back? Tell father and mother, then all go trading post."

Evelyn shook her head. "The idea is to catch him before something happens. Horses don't last long in the mountains on their own. Too many accidents waiting to happen. Too many meat-eaters with a hankering for horse flesh."

Dega had not thought of that.

"Then there are other whites and Indians to think of. Anyone who spots him will want him for their own, and if they catch him, they are not likely to give him up without a scrape."

"But it our horse."

"You know that and I know that, but try telling a Blackfoot or a Piegan they can't keep a horse they just caught and they are as likely as not to try and turn you into a pincushion. To them, if an animal is wandering free, then it is anybody's to claim. You will have to kiss your horse goodbye or kill them to get it back."

"I not kill men over horse."

"You will have to change that attitude right quick if you want to last out here. What is yours is yours, and no one has the right to take it from you. But don't you worry. If someone does get hold of the dun, my pa will do whatever it takes to get him back."

"Your father kill?"

"Only if he has to." Evelyn reined to the right to avoid a boulder. "Now if my brother Zach shows up, then it is a whole different story. He will walk up to whoever has your horse, stick a pistol to their head, and tell them they have two choices." She smiled fondly. "Zach isn't one for pussyfooting around. They will hand it over or they will die."

There was something about Zach King, a ferocity lurking just under the surface, that Dega had to admit he found disturbing. Zach seemed to revel in conflict and combat. Dega understood that part of it was due to the Shoshone custom of counting coup on enemies. Like many tribes in the region, the Shoshones gauged valor by how many coup a man could claim. The more coup, the more esteemed the warrior.

It was not a new concept. Tribes in the region where the Nansusequa had lived did the same.

But not the Nansusequa. To them, the most esteemed warriors were those with the wisdom to smooth over conflicts and avoid bloodshed. Peace was their standard, not war. Oh, they would defend themselves when they had to, with a savagery to match their foes. But only when forced. Only when those who had raised arms against them would not be pacified.

Evelyn avoided more boulders. She also marked the position of the sun. At most they had three hours of daylight left. "We should start to keep our eyes skinned for a place to camp."

"So soon?"

"Buttercup is about tuckered out. I'll keep going until dark if I have to, but if we find a spot sooner, so much the better. We will make an early start in the morning and hopefully you will be riding the dun by the end of the day."

"What you think best, we do," Dega said.

"You are learning," Evelyn grinned. "My pa says that one of the most important lessons for a man to learn is that women are always right."

"Always?"

"As near to it as counts. Or with your people do the men actually wear the britches?"

He had been doing so well, he thought. But once again Dega had no idea what she was talking about. *Britches* was a white word for pants. Nansusequa women always wore dresses. Nor had he ever seen Winona King in pants. "Wear britches important?"

"To some it is. My pa likes to joke that once he took my ma to be his wife, he had to give all the pants he owns to her. But my pa is a great josher."

This made even less sense to Dega, since Nate King was a giant whose clothes would never fit Winona. "She give dresses to him?"

Evelyn squealed with glee. "Mercy me, no! But wouldn't that be a sight? My pa in a <u>dress</u>! I'll have to remember to tell my brother that one. It will give him a kick."

"A kick is good?"

"It means to make them laugh." Evelyn spied a ridge below, and the blue of flowing water. "Look yonder! We might be in luck. If that's a stream, we've found our spot to camp."

Dega hefted his lance. "I hunt if you want."

The trees thinned, affording their first clear view of the country they had entered. Before them stretched a winding valley choked with timber. To the north and south towered imposing peaks, a few crowned with snow.

Evelyn stiffened and rose in the stirrups. "Do

my eyes deceive me or is that what I think it is? Look there." She pointed to the east.

Dega accounted himself keen of sight, but he strained and beheld only trees. He said as much.

"Look again. To the right of that real tall pine. It comes and it goes." Evelyn pointed. "There it is again!"

This time Dega saw what she saw.

Tendrils of smoke from a campfire.

Chapter Ten

Evelyn was not the judge of distance her father was. She reckoned the smoke was three miles away, but she could be off by half a mile or more. "Whoever it is, we're lucky we spotted them before they spotted us."

"Maybe white men," Dega said. Since the slaughter of his people, he regarded all whites with the deepest suspicion. Nearly all; the exceptions were the King family and the McNairs.

"I don't think so," Evelyn said. The general rule of thumb for campfires was that if it was a big one, then whites made it, and if it was a small one, nine times out of ten Indians were responsible. This one was not giving off much smoke. "More likely they are Indians."

"Friendly or hostile?" Degamawaku asked.

"I can't predict," Evelyn said. To the best of her knowledge the surrounding countryside was not claimed by any particular tribe. The campfire could belong to warriors from any of half a dozen: Blackfeet, Crows, Nez Perce, the Utes, even her mother's people, the Shoshones.

"We go see?"

Evelyn was tempted. It might simply be a hunting party of friendly Indians. Then again, it could be a war party, in which case she dared not risk the warriors finding out they were there. "It's best we leave them be. In the morning they'll likely move on and we can get on with our search for your dun."

"What we do now?"

"What do you think?" Evelyn rejoined, and reined into the timber. "Look for a spot to camp."

Near the north end of the ridge, on the side opposite the distant smoke, was a bowl-shaped depression half an acre in size.

"This will do nicely," Evelyn said, and made for the center. She was pleasantly surprised to find a small spring, the surface glistening like a polished mirror. Tracks testified to its popularity, but none of the prints, Evelyn was pleased to note, were human. Whoever was down in the valley was apparently unaware of the spring.

Dega took his lance and went in search of game. He did not have to go far. As he came to the west rim of the hollow, he spooked a rabbit. It took three long bounds, then made a mistake common to small game: it stopped to look back to see if he was giving chase. He wasn't. He did not need to when he had his lance. The point caught the rabbit in the side.

Evelyn saw his cast. She was making their fire, but had been watching him. The throw impressed her. A Shoshone could not have done it better.

Dega carried the rabbit back by its ears. Drawing his knife, he squatted. He inserted the tip and cut a slit down the center of the belly and along the inside of each leg. Then he deftly peeled off the skin, chopped off the head, removed the guts, and impaled the body on a stick.

Evelyn had seen her father and her brother do the same countless times, but she found it especially interesting to watch Degamawaku. Everything he did was of interest to her, stemming, she felt, from the fact that he was from a tribe so far removed from those she knew. She liked to compare how he did things to how the Shoshones did things. There were many similarities. There were also quite a few differences.

Accepting the spit, Evelyn rigged it over the fire. She had kept it small. Sheltered as they were by the hollow, she rated the prospect of it being spotted as slim.

The aroma of the roasting meat made her mouth water and her tummy growl.

"You much hungry," Dega teased.

"That I am," Evelyn admitted. It had been a long day and tomorrow promised to be more of the same. Her big worry was that the dun had waltzed into the camp of whoever was down the valley, and they would want to keep it for themselves.

Dega wrapped his arms around his knees and stared at the rabbit. Otherwise, he would stare at her. "It do smell good."

"This is the first time we have ever been out alone together at night," Evelyn remarked.

"Yes."

"I trust you will be a perfect gentleman," Evelyn said light-heartedly. He had never been anything but.

Dega pieced together her meaning. He had heard *gentleman* used before; whites used it as another word for *man*. 'Perfect,' as he understood it, had to do with not having a blemish, or being without flaw. She was saying, he concluded, that she expected him to be a flawless man, but how exactly he was supposed to go about doing that, he couldn't begin to guess.

"You never talk much about what your life was like back where you came from," Evelyn said.

"Sad to talk. Hurt here," Dega said, and pressed his hand to his chest over his heart.

"I savvy," Evelyn responded. But there was something she very much wanted to know, something she had held off asking for weeks now. "Did you have a gal friend?"

"A what?" Dega knew *gal* was another word for girl, and he knew friend, but the combination was new to him.

"A girl you were fond of. Someone you were close to. Someone you might have married one day."

"Oh. No," Dega answered. "I have many friends who be girls, but not that way."

"I was just curious," Evelyn said, trying to justify her interest. "I've never had a man friend I felt that way about, either."

"You will," Dega assured her.

"What makes you say that?"

"You pretty. You fun. You nice be with," Dega said. "Any man be happy have you."

"Why, thank you." Evelyn shifted uncomfortably. "But I'm not in any great hurry to become hitched. I would as soon be my own woman another five or ten years before I say 'I do.'"

"Ten winters?" Dega repeated, aghast. It struck him as a terribly long time.

"Give or take," Evelyn said. "But you never know. A handsome prince might come along and sweep me off my feet."

"A what?" This was another new term.

"A prince. They are in fairy tales and stories like that. The perfect man, every girl's dream."

Dega was confused, yet again. Had she not said just a short while ago that she expected *him* to behave as a perfect man? Did that mean he was a prince?

"In real life there aren't any, of course," Evelyn rambled on. "More's the pity, as Shakespeare would say."

"No princes?" Dega said. But hadn't she remarked that there were? Which was it?

"They are make-believe. Although, if you ask my ma, she will say my pa is her prince. And if you ask Louisa, she will say my brother, Zach, is hers. Which goes to show she wasn't very choosy."

"Sorry?"

"There are princes, and there are princes. They can't all be charming through and through."

Dega scratched his head in bewilderment. At times like this he despaired of ever understanding the white tongue. Then he looked at Evelyn and resolved to try harder. "Charming be good?"

"Most women think so, yes."

"Am I any charming?"

"Some," Evelyn allowed. But what she was thinking was that he was the most charming person she had ever met.

The fire crackled noisily. Teak had added green wood instead of dead wood, and it had started to give off a lot of smoke.

Rafer Bodin coughed, then growled in irritation, "Can't you do anything right?"

"I didn't get the wrong wood on purpose," Teak said. "No need to raise a stink about it."

"The idea is not to advertise we're here," Bodin said. "You might want to remember that."

Mandingo was the only one still eating. There was not much left of the fawn Graf had shot, but what there was Mandingo would devour. He never let meat go to waste. It came from a childhood of near starvation. "You two are always at each other's throats."

"I'll be at it for real if he doesn't stop trying my patience," Bodin said. "Graf and you don't give me half the sass he does."

"I give no sass," Graf said.

Teak leaned back and picked at his teeth with a twig. "I can't help it if I speak my mind. I wasn't born to be a doorstep, like some. I don't ask how high when I'm told to jump. I ask why."

Graf rose on an elbow, his features twisted in anger. "Do you insult me again?"

"All I'm saying is that I think for myself. If some here don't like that, then maybe I should go my own way." Teak paused. "After we divvy up what we get from the furs, of course."

"Keep on as you are and maybe you won't get

anything," Bodin said. He was sorry he ever let the chronic complainer join them. But then, men who liked to kill and steal as much as he did were hard to find. He could not be choosy.

"That would not be fair," Teak said. "That would not be fair at all."

"Life is not about fair," Bodin shot back. "It's about taking what you want when you want, and everyone else be damned."

Mandingo stopped chewing. "Does that include us?"

Bodin sensed the accusation. "Listen, you've been with me long enough to know I always share the spoils. Have I ever once shorted you or Graf?"

"No," Graf said. "You're the most honest man I know."

Teak laughed.

"What's so funny?" Graf asked.

"If I say, you'll only be mad, so I won't say." Teak shifted toward Bodin. "I still don't savvy why we didn't take the furs straight to Bent's Fort. Why ride around with them for a month before we get rid of them?"

"I've explained it already," Bodin said irritably. "If we wait, it's less likely there will be friends of those Crows we killed hanging around the trading post."

"Hell, they were alone. We proved that by spying on them. You're as cautious as an old woman."

"I'm alive," Bodin said.

"A whole month, though," Teak griped. "If you want to be shed of me, why don't we turn around and dispose of the furs. I'll take my share and go my way."

"I said a month, and a month it will be."

"Then you'll have to put up with my company that much longer," Teak said, and grinned. "Aren't you the lucky ones?"

"Talk, talk, talk," Graf grumbled. "You couldn't keep quiet for five minutes if your life depended on it."

Mandingo was sucking the marrow from a bone. "What I want to know is how long we will stay in this country? We have not seen a soul since those Crows."

"I like it like that," Bodin said. "I never have been fond of people." Most, like Teak, were a trial.

"Neither have I," the mulatto said. "But fewer people means less we can help ourselves to. The pickings will be slim."

"We will help ourselves to what we can, when we can," Bodin said. "White, red, young, old, it makes no nevermind. We take what they have, whether it is a little or a lot, and bury them."

Teak was about to add another piece of wood to the fire. "That's another thing. Why do you always make us plant them? Why not leave the bodies to rot? It would be easier."

"They're less apt to be found if they're buried. Or are you fond of the idea of having your neck stretched?"

Motioning at the forest, Teak said, "I could see it back in the States where there are people everywhere. But out here in the middle of nowhere, who is there to find them?"

"Lightning only has to strike but once," Bodin reminded him.

"You're he-coon of this bunch," Teak said. "So

do we ride around in circles for a month or do you aim to go somewhere?"

"We'll scout out these mountains," Bodin said, "and be on the lookout for settlers."

"I hope we find us a woman soon," Graf mentioned. "I don't like to go long without."

"Me either, my friend," Mandingo said. "That one with the wagon, she sure was fine. I was almost sorry to strangle her."

"There is more to life than women," Teak said.

"Not for me," Mandingo said. "I like killing, and I'd rather steal than work for a living, but I do this for the women more than anything. To take a female by force is the pleasure of pleasures."

"My pleasure is whiskey," Teak said, "which I have not had enough of since I joined this outfit."

"Don't start on that again," Bodin warned. He glanced at their horses, then off into the night to the west. Suddenly rising, he peered hard into the darkness. "Did any of you see that?"

"What?" Graf asked.

"For a second there I thought I saw the light from a campfire, but now it's gone." Bodin stared a while, then sat back down. "In the morning we should go see. It could be more easy pickings."

"Just so long as there is a woman," Mandingo said, and smacked his lips. "Young and pretty, the way I like them."

√

Chapter Eleven

Maybe it was her full belly, or maybe it was the warmth of the fire, or both, but Evelyn had seldom felt so at peace, so content, as she did sitting there listening to Degamawaku talk about his childhood. She learned that while the Nansusequa called themselves the People of the Forest, neighboring tribes had referred to them as the Old Ones. Not because the Nansusequa lived to an extremely old age—although many did—but because they had been the first tribe to live in that region. Indeed, according to their own legends, they were the first tribe ever created. But other tribes had similar legends.

In contrast to the Shoshones, to whom counting coup was the measure of a warrior, the Nansusequa had devoted themselves to peaceful pursuits. To their way of thinking, war was an act of last resort. Warriors were esteemed for their devotion to That Which Is In All Things.

It gave Evelyn much to ponder. Every tribe she

knew of counted coup; the Blackfeet, the Sioux, the Cheyenne, the Utes, the Flatheads. To them, most every other tribe was an enemy, to be attacked on sight.

Not the Nansusequa. "We try live in peace with everyone," Dega said, the firelight playing over his handsome features.

"That would not be practical out here," Evelyn commented. "Some tribes don't care how peaceful you are. They will kill you anyway."

"Whites did the same," Dega mentioned, clouding at the memory. He wondered if he would ever forget that terrible day.

"I am sorry for what you went through," Evelyn said. "But not all whites are like those from New Albion. Some of us don't think the only good Indian is a dead Indian."

"You be special," Dega said.

"Oh, I wouldn't say that. A lot of whites are peaceable."

"No. I mean *you*." Of all the whites Dega ever met, only she made his pulse quicken and his thoughts stray in troubling ways.

"I am flattered," Evelyn said. She stared into the fire and grew warm but not from the flames. "You say the nicest things sometimes."

For a while neither spoke. Then Dega said, "Tell me. You really wait ten winters to share lodge with man?"

"Maybe not quite that long," Evelyn conceded. "But I'm young yet. I see no reason to rush." In the past year she had discouraged two suitors and had no hankering to have another.

"Among my people," Dega said, "man must court woman four seasons."

"A full year? What if the two people want to become husband and wife sooner?"

"Four seasons," Dega reiterated. "That way both be sure. They stay together."

For some reason Evelyn felt vaguely uncomfortable talking about marriage. Which struck her as odd since as she had made it plain she had no interest in wedlock and would not have any interest for a good many years yet. She got Dega to talk about his family instead, and listened to the love in his voice as he described how caring and devoted they were. He was deeply fond of his sisters.

"I would never admit it to him," she remarked when he was done, "but I reckon I feel the same about my brother. We spat a lot, but there is no one I would rather have for a brother than Zach."

The idea of love growing out of conflict was a new notion to Dega. He had been taught that love grew out of harmony, that when two people genuinely cared for one another, they did not fight or raise their voice or do any of the things Evelyn seemed to take for granted as normal.

The hour was late, the fire dwindling, when Evelyn asked her final question of the night. "What do you want to do with your life?"

"Live," Dega said.

Evelyn laughed. "No, silly. I mean, what is your goal in life? There must be something you want to do more than anything else?"

"To take wife, to have children," Dega answered honestly. Just as his father had done, and his father's father, and on back the family line to the beginning.

"What kind of wife?"

"There be kinds?"

"Sure. Tall, short, quiet, outgoing. What traits do you look for most of all? What traits don't you like?"

Dega considered carefully, choosing the right words so in this there would be no mistake. "I want woman who be—" he caught himself. "Sorry. I want woman who is pure of heart."

Evelyn waited, and when he did not go on, she said, "That's it?"

"That is it."

"But what does that mean, exactly? You want a woman who has never been with a man, is that it?" Evelyn felt herself blushing as she added, "What white men call a virgin."

"That not so important as pure of heart," Dega said.

"Explain to me the difference," Evelyn requested. "I would really like to know."

Once again Dega tried to be exact. "You know Mississippi River?"

"I have seen it several times," Evelyn said. "I even fell in it once. But what does that have to do with anything?"

"Mississippi is dirty river. Water brown. Can not see bottom when stand on bank."

"That is why some folks call it Big Muddy. So?"

"So lake we live near not like Mississippi," Dega said. "Lake clear. Can see bottom." He looked for the light of comprehension in her lovely green eyes but did not see it. "I want woman with heart like lake, not like Mississippi. I want woman with heart that be pure."

Evelyn looked inward at her own heart. "How can you tell?" she asked. "It is not as if you can see into a person's heart just by looking at her."

"Yes, can," Dega disagreed. He raised a hand and held two fingers close to his eyes. "You look here."

"Ah." Evelyn wrapped her forearms around her legs and shammed an interest in the stars. She wanted to ask him whether her heart was like the lake or the Mississippi, but she was afraid of his answer.

Shortly after, they turned in. Evelyn curled on her side with a blanket up to her chin and her saddle for a pillow. Her eyes not quite shut, she watched him make himself comfortable on his back and fold his hands on his chest. He did not use a blanket.

Evelyn was tired from the long hours on horseback and figured she would go right to sleep. But her mind was racing like a Chinook. She could not stop thinking about the things they had talked about. She tossed. She turned. She tried counting sheep, as her father advised her to do when she was little. Dega appeared to be slumbering peacefully. She envied him. If she did not get some rest, she would pay for it the next day. Upset with herself, she turned her back to the fire and tried to empty her head of all thoughts.

Dega heard her turn over and glanced in her direction. From where he lay, she seemed to be sleeping. He wished he could. He kept reliving the day in his mind. Or, rather, reliving all that she had said and done. Every gesture she made, every comment. He relived everything they did from the moment he arrived at the King cabin until they turned in. It was a day he would treasure, for no matter what happened in the future, they had had this one day to themselves. He thanked That Which Is In All Things for being able to share it with her.

Evelyn finally started to drift off. She was on the cusp of dreamland when the screech of an owl snapped her awake. Clamping her jaw in frustration, she mentally cursed owls in general and that one in particular.

Sleep came at long last. Evelyn had the impression she barely drifted off when a jay squawked and the sky was brightening. She slowly sat up, her blood sluggish in her veins, and yawned. Another night like this and she would be a wreck. To her surprise, Dega was already up.

Dega had not slept at all. He had tried and tried and given it up as hopeless. In the quiet, still time before dawn, he lay listening to Evelyn breathe and imagined how it would be to do that the rest of his life.

They were underway before the sun was half an hour high. Evelyn rode up out of the bowl to the top of the ridge. At the far end of the valley smoke curled above the treetops. Whoever it was, they were having their breakfast.

"We will go easy until we find out if they are friend or foe," Evelyn said.

Sticking to cover, stopping often to listen and look, Evelyn crossed the heavily forested valley floor. As they neared the smoke she expected to hear voices, but the woods were silent and still. When the smell of the smoke was so strong she was sure they were close, she drew rein. Dega slid down and then she dismounted and wrapped the reins around a sapling. Her rifle at the ready, she cautiously advanced to the edge of a clearing.

The fire was almost out, its makers gone. Hoofprints and footprints indicated seven riders with three pack animals had camped overnight. The fletching and marks on a broken arrow they had left told Evelyn it had been a Nez Perce hunting party. They had gone off toward their own country.

"We find tracks of dun now?" Dega asked.

It took some doing. Evelyn thought the horse would make for the Nez Perce camp, but it had given them a wide berth. By roving in a circle, she found its trail leading toward the far end the valley. It was still heading lower, toward the foothills and eventually Bent's Fort.

Evelyn rode hard, but Buttercup was bearing double and she had to stop often to let the buttermilk rest. They did not catch up that day. They did not catch up the next. She knew her parents would be worried, but she refused to give up. She had come this far; she would keep going all the way to the trading post if she had to. That it was Dega's horse was added incentive.

Dega did not care how long it took. He relished being in Evelyn's company. During the day they traveled through spectacular terrain, with towering peaks on all sides. At night they sat around their campfire and talked until they could not keep their eyes open.

A third day waxed and waned. Once again they camped. As Evelyn was stripping Buttercup, she spotted a campfire in the distance.

"Nez Perce, you think?"

"No," Evelyn answered. "They were heading northwest. That fire is to the southeast. And it is a lot bigger than the fire the Nez Perce made. My guess would be white men. We'll go have a look in the morning."

"You think they have dun?" Dega's grasp of the white tongue was improving. He had reached the point where he sometimes thought in it.

"Maybe. Maybe not. It won't hurt to see."

That night they talked of all the things they had in common. They both grew up in loving families. They both had devoted, caring parents. Much of their lives had been spent outdoors. They liked the beauty of nature. Neither cared for violence.

Dega asked her if she believed in Manitoa, as did he and all his family, and Evelyn explained about God and the Bible. Dega was greatly interested in the story of the man who died on the cross. He did not understand much of it, but he gathered that the man had a deep, abiding love for others, and he wondered if the God of the whites and the Manitoa of his people might be one and the same.

"That I can't say," Evelyn replied. "I never gave religion a lot of thought. You might ask my pa. He reads the Bible all the time, and he likes to mull over questions like that." She poked the fire with a stick. "Me, I used to think that God watches over us and keeps us from harm. That was before I was kidnapped and some terrible things happened to those I care for most. Now I don't know."

"We not blame That Which Is In All Things for all that bad," Dega remarked.

"Why not? If God made this world, then He is responsible for everyone and everything in it— the good as well as the bad." At least, that was how Evelyn saw it. "But what do I know? I gave up looking for answers a long time ago."

"Never give up," Dega said.

"Some things just don't make any sense no matter how hard I think about them."

Dega was struck by how much older she was inside than outside. The hardships she had suffered had matured her beyond her years.

"Enough about the meaning of life." Evelyn grinned. "It's getting late. We should turn in so we're bright-eyed and bushy-tailed when we go see who's camped yonder in the morning."

Dega was not looking forward to that. He liked having her to himself. But he did not say anything, and soon she was breathing deeply and regularly in peaceful sleep. He drifted off himself soon after.

The day broke cloudy and dreary. Evelyn sniffed the air and announced what Dega had already deduced. "We will have rain today."

Evelyn was in no hurry. She dallied over strips of rabbit meat left over from the night before. She took her sweet time saddling Buttercup. She rode at a leisurely walk through the gray and gloomy woods. The dun's tracks pointed straight toward the other camp. "It could be you will get your horse back soon," she commented.

"That be good," Dega fibbed. He was not delighted at the prospect of heading back to their own valley and their families. He should have been, but he was not.

"Yes, it is," Evelyn said, sounding as excited about it as he did.

"I thank you for coming all this way for my horse," Dega said, delighted at how well he spoke.

"We don't have him yet," Evelyn noted.

The trees thinned. Ahead, in a clearing, men were moving about, evidently preparing to get underway.

"I count four," Dega said.

So did Evelyn. She studied them. As she had suspected, they were white. Or three of them were. One was sandy-haired, another was short and constantly scowled, a third bulged with muscle, while the fourth was a mix of white and black—a mulatto, she believed they were called.

Evelyn rode to the edge of the clearing and drew rein. Raising an arm, she called out, "Hallo, the camp!"

Instantly, the four men whirled and brandished weapons. On seeing her, the short one smiled and declared, "As I live and breathe, boys! Look at what we have here."

"Do you mind if we have words with you?" Evelyn asked.

"Not at all, girl," the short one responded, and lowered his rifle. "Come on in. I am Rafer Bodin and these are my pards, Graf, Mandingo and Teak. We'll be right pleased to make your acquaintance."

Chapter Twelve

Evelyn kneed Buttercup closer but stopped after only going a few yards. She did not like how the four men were looking at her. They were all smiling as if they were as friendly as could be, but something about their smiles rang false. Her intuition blared. That, and her father and mother warning her time and time again never to trust strangers until the strangers proved trustworthy. "We're looking for a horse that ran away," she informed them. "A zebra dun. Have you seen it by any chance?"

Bodin placed the stock of his rifle on the ground and leaned on it. He didn't want to do anything that would scare the girl and the Indian boy off. He was pleased to see the others had caught on and were acting as peaceable as parsons. "Can't say as we have, girl. But why don't you light and rest a spell? We have coffee on."

Degamawaku did not trust the four whites. Their faces reminded him of the faces of the whites from New Albion who destroyed his village and his people. Leaning forward, he whispered to Evelyn, "These not good men."

Bodin saw him whisper. "What was that, Injun? I didn't quite catch what you said."

"It is his horse that ran away," Evelyn said. "He is anxious to find it." She noticed a pair of pack animals laden with furs. "I see you are trappers."

"Eh?" Bodin said, and followed her gaze. "That we are. On our way to Bent's Fort to trade our hides. You're welcome to join us if you'd like."

"We must find the dun."

Bodin rose onto the tips of his toes and stared past them. "Is there just the two of you, girl? Where are your folks?"

"Close by," Evelyn lied. "They are searching for the horse."

"Is that a fact?" Bodin almost laughed. "You're a terrible liar. Or do you expect me to believe they don't mind you riding around alone with that buck?"

"He is my friend," Evelyn said, angered by the insult. "And I will thank you not to talk like that."

"No offense meant, pretty thing," Bodin said. He flicked his eyes meaningfully at the others. Mandingo immediately started to move to the right and Graf to the left, but slowly, so as not to be obvious about it.

Evelyn raised her rifle. "Hold it right there. I don't know what you're up to, but I'll shoot if you make me."

"Have a care, girl," Bodin said good-naturedly. "What is this talk of shooting? What have we done other than offer you some coffee and the comfort of our fire?"

Evelyn centered the barrel on his chest and thumbed back the hammer. "I mean it. Tell your friends to stand still, or you won't like the consequences."

Bodin gestured, stopping Mandingo and Graf. "Now see here," he declared, "I can't say much for your manners."

"You strike me as unsavory," Evelyn bluntly informed him. "If I am wrong, I apologize. But my friend and I will be on our way, and no one had better try to stop us."

"We wouldn't think of it, young lady," Bodin assured her. "Go in peace."

Evelyn gigged Buttercup in a loop that brought her around to the other side of the clearing. The whole time she pointed her rifle at Bodin. Neither he nor the others tried to stop them. About to rein into the pines, she remarked, "As you said to me, no offense meant. We bid you good day, gentlemen." A jab of her heels brought Buttercup to a trot.

Teak was nearly beside himself. "Why in hell did you let them get away?" he demanded. "We should have jumped them while we had the chance."

"And take lead in the bargain? You saw that girl. She was no bluff. She's worth her weight in gold, that one."

"I saw her, all right," Mandingo said, and licked his lips. "I can not wait to have her."

"I want to choke that Injun she is with," Graf said. "If there's anything I hate worse than Injuns, I have yet to find it."

"We are going after them, aren't we?" Teak asked. "We can't let a saucy vixen like her slip through our fingers."

"And we won't," Bodin said. "But we will go slow and do this right so she is not harmed when we jump them." He rubbed his palms together in glee. "Mandingo and Graf, mount up. We have us some rabbits to snare."

"What about me?" Teak asked.

"You stay here and watch the pack animals," Bodin instructed. "We should be back by nightfall."

"How come I have to stay?" Teak objected. "Why not Mandingo?"

"He can track and you can't."

"Graf, then."

"You're not half as strong as he is, and there's liable to be a scrape when we jump them."

"You make me sound next to worthless," Teak groused.

"You are."

A hundred yards into the forest, Evelyn had slowed her horse to a walk. Twisting, she scanned their back trail. "I don't see them," she said. "Maybe I was mistaken and they were harmless."

"You did right thing," Dega said. "Nansusequa have saying." He translated it in his head. "A wolf cannot bite you if you are not near it."

"Whites have a saying, too," Evelyn said. "Better safe than sorry." She glanced back from time to time, but no one was after them. Overhead, the clouds darkened. The wind picked up, bringing with it the scent of the rain she had predicted.

"Storm come soon," Dega said.

"It will erase the dun's sign," Evelyn mentioned. "We'll have to go all the way to Bent's Fort and hope it's there."

"I not mind." Dega looked forward to spending more time in her company. The dun had done him a favor.

"Me either," Evelyn said.

"Hold on a moment," Evelyn said, drawing rein. She had glanced back again and this time she saw something. "Open that parfleche and hand me the spyglass."

Dega complied, extending it as he gave it to her. Shifting, he asked, "What back there?"

"Don't move," Evelyn said. She rested the end of the telescope on his shoulder to steady it and looked through the eyepiece. "I was right. It's the one who called himself Bodin. He is smack on our trail."

"The others?"

Evelyn swung the spyglass from side to side. Her insides churned as she spotted the mulatto to the south and the mass of muscle to the north. "Two of them are coming up on either side. They must reckon to flank us, then close in." She snapped the spyglass shut. "I was right about them. They're up to no good."

"You think they want our guns and Buttercup?

"It could be they want me." Evelyn lashed her reins. "Hang on." At a gallop they raced through the woods, while around them the trees bent to the force of the rising wind and dark clouds scuttled like so many giant crabs. The scent of moisture was stronger than ever.

Dega clung on, his worry for Evelyn eclipsing all else. It never would have occurred to him that the men were after her. Violating a woman was so despicable, so vile, it went against everything the Nansusequa believed.

The forest had gone quiet save for the drum of Buttercup's hooves. No birds sang; no squirrels chattered. The wild things had sensed the impending storm and sought their dens and burrows and nests.

Evelyn was surprised at how calm she felt. She told herself that she had no reason to be overly worried. She had her weapons, and Dega had his lance. Between them they could give a good accounting of themselves.

Buttercup was layered with sweat when Evelyn finally drew rein. By then the sky was so dark, it almost seemed to be night. She used the spyglass, sweeping the timber behind them. "I don't see them. I think we got away."

"I hope you be right," Dega said.

A few cold drops spattered Evelyn's face. "We must find shelter from the rain." Quickly, she closed the telescope and handed it to Dega. "Put that in the parfleche."

A sudden howl of wind whipped the trees. Evelyn took the reins and used her heels. Ahead rose the slopes of yet another mountain.

Dega did not share her urgency. Rain was rain. He had been caught in storms many times. The worst that could happen was they would be soaked to the skin.

A distant flash of light was followed by a rumbling boom.

"Lightning. Just what we need," Evelyn said, her tone full of sarcasm. Storms in the mountains could be incredibly fierce.

Dega wondered if the men who were chasing them were as concerned about the storm as she was. If so, they might give up and find a spot to wait it out.

The buttermilk headed up an incline.

Evelyn bent and spoke softly. "That's it, girl. Just a little farther. I am sorry for pushing you like this, but it can't be helped." She patted Buttercup's neck.

Another flash, brighter than the last, was attended by a louder rumble. Some of the thinner pines were practically bent double.

Dega twisted to look behind them. The shadows themselves seemed to dance and writhe. He did not see their three pursuers anywhere. He smiled. Then the lightning blazed again and he thought he saw—something—at the limit of his vision. It was there, and it was gone. It might have been an animal. But he was filled with unease.

Evelyn spied a break in the terrain to their left and angled toward it. Out of the murk a gully appeared. The sides were not steep and the bottom was littered with gravel. It was not much, but it would have to do. She reined down into it. "We will wait out the storm here."

"Whatever you want," Dega said. It was a good place to hide. But he did not like that they could not see over the top.

Dismounting, Evelyn held firmly to the reins. She was not going to be stranded afoot a second time.

The scattered drops became a drizzle. Here in the gully the wind seemed louder. It keened and shrieked and buffeted them nonstop.

Evelyn hunched against Buttercup, her chin tucked low. She did not like getting wet unless she was taking a bath. It had been a pet peeve of hers since childhood. Her brother once teased that she must be part chicken, since when it rained, the chickens huddled in their coop and clucked irritably. *You must have hatched out of an egg*, Zach had said with a grin. *I can't wait to see you flap your wings and fly.* He was always saying silly things like that. God, how she wished he were there. Zach would ride up to those men and shoot them dead and that would be the end of it.

A vivid streak rent the heavens, and a tree not a hundred yards away was blasted in twain. The thunder was deafening.

Buttercup whinnied and shied, and it was all Evelyn could do to hold her. "There, there," she said, stroking her horse's neck. "Take it easy. I'm here. I won't let anything happen to you."

"What I do to help?" Dega asked.

"Hold on to the bridle," Evelyn said. Buttercup might shake one of them off but not both.

Dega did so, and smiled. "Next time I want see mountain sheep, beat me with rock."

Evelyn laughed. She appreciated that he was being so helpful and considerate. "You sure are something, you know that."

Dega worked that out in his head. Of course he was something; he was a person. Was there more to it? "Am I good something?"

"Very good," Evelyn said, and looked down at the ground so he would not notice her expression.

With a tremendous crash and a screech, the storm unleashed it full fury. The rain became a deluge, the wind an invisible behemoth that pummeled the earth mercilessly. Except for the lightning flashes, the sky was as black as pitch.

Evelyn could not see her hand in front of her face. She held her Hawken in front of her, pressed close, trying to keep it from getting wet.

Dega had never experienced a storm like this. The rain was ice cold. The wind whipped his breath away. The din from the thunder assaulted his ears. He recalled Shakespeare McNair saying once that the weather in the mountains was more severe than in the lowlands. McNair had been right.

Evelyn lost all track of time. It might have been an hour, it might have been longer, when she detected a lessening of the downpour. The clouds went from black to gray. She was further encouraged when the wind momentarily died. The worst was about over.

That was when Evelyn heard a sound she could not account for. A rumbling different from the thunder. It came from the mountain above. She gazed up the gully, perplexed. The sound troubled her. She felt that she should know what it was.

"What that be?" Dega asked.

"Maybe a rock slide high up," Evelyn speculated.

The next instant a roiling, seething wall of water twenty feet high came hurtling around a bend, sweeping away everything before it.

Chapter Thirteen

Flash flood.

How many times had Evelyn's father warned her about them? In the mountains, sudden rainstorms had the potential to transform every dry wash, gully, ravine and gorge into raging rivers in the blink of an eye. Many an unwary animal, and careless human, had found that out the fatal way.

Now, as the seething wall of water bore down on them, Evelyn knew they would not get out of the gully in time. She frantically tugged on the reins but Buttercup could not climb the slippery slope fast enough. In seconds the water would reach them. Her eyes met Dega's. He was pulling on the bridle, trying to help. "Run!" she cried. "Save yourself!"

Dega did the opposite. He reached for her hand. "Get behind horse," he said, refusing to abandon her.

Barely were the words out of his mouth when

the wall of water slammed into them. Buttercup squealed as she was swept off her hooves.

Evelyn tried to hold on to Dega but the brutal force of the water ripped her from him even as she was lifted off her feet and propelled down the gully as if shot from a canon. A liquid cocoon enfolded her. She managed to suck in a breath of air, and then she was under water and flung with irresistible force like a twig in a torrent. End over end she tumbled, losing all sense of up and down. Rocks and limbs struck her again and again. A boulder half as big as Buttercup went hurtling past her head. She lost sight of Buttercup, and of Dega. The roar of the flood filled her ears, the water filled her nose and seeped into her mouth. Her lungs strained for air, but she grit her teeth and willed her mouth to stay shut.

A tree loomed, and she narrowly missed it. It meant the water had carried her out of the gully and into the forest. At any moment she might be dashed to pieces. She twisted, trying to swim, but the water would not be denied. She was helpless, at the mercy of capricious fate.

Evelyn thought of her father and mother, and of Zach. She might never see them again. Her father would find her body, of that she was sure. She was sorry for them, sorry that she would cause them sorrow.

She glimpsed something in front of her. Another tree, maybe. Before she could react, she smashed into it. Pain racked her. Then came a blow to the head, and the brown of the water began to fade to black.

I am dying, Evelyn thought.

Then there was nothing.

Her first sensation was of warmth on her face.

Evelyn opened her eyes and blinked against the glare of the late afternoon sun. She went to turn her head and almost cried out. A throbbing pain reminded her of what had happened. Gingerly, carefully, she looked to each side.

She was on her back in a field of mud. Here and there were pools and puddles of water. The clouds were gone; the sky was clear. She had been out for hours.

Ever so slowly, Evelyn rose onto her elbows and looked down at herself. Her dress was soaked and caked with mud and bits of grass and leaves. She still had her ammo pouch and powder horn, but her pistols and her knife were gone. She moved one leg and then the other. Nothing appeared broken, but she hurt in several places.

Something was poking her in the back. Evelyn eased to one side, and grinned. She had been lying on her rifle. At least she had a gun, even if it would be of no use to her until it dried out and she reloaded.

"Dega?" Evelyn sat up. He was nowhere to be seen. Neither was Buttercup. Apparently she had been swept through the trees and deposited in a meadow. They might not have been as lucky. She started to stand, but her legs were wobbly. Reluctantly, she sat back down to wait for her strength to return.

Evelyn bowed her head and closed her eyes.

Everything that could go wrong had gone wrong, but she must not give in to panic. Her parents had taught her better than that. She must stay clam and do what needed doing, and she would make it out alive.

Belatedly, Evelyn became aware of the *plop-plop* of heavy hooves in the mud. She glanced up, startled, and started to push to her feet.

"Stay right where you are, girl," Mandingo said, training the muzzle of his rifle on her. "I do not want to shoot you so do not give me cause."

Evelyn clenched her fists and glared. To be caught like this, weak and defenseless, made her furious. "What do you want?"

"I think you know," the mulatto said, and smiled a lecherous smile. "I love the pretty ones, and you are very pretty."

"Go to hell," Evelyn said.

Mandingo laughed. "No doubt I will. But not before I have tasted many more treats such as you."

"I will scratch out your eyes. I will rip out your throat with my teeth."

Reining up, Mandingo swung a leg over one side and sat there in his saddle. "Sorry to disappoint you, little one, but you won't have the chance. You're ours to do with as we please."

Evelyn scanned the meadow. He was alone. "Where are your friends?"

"We separated to search for you and the Indian," Mandingo revealed. "We lost track of you in the storm." He placed a hand on a flintlock tucked under his belt. "Now I will signal them. They will come quick. They're as eager as I am to partake of your charms."

"I have never been with a man." Evelyn did not know why she said that. She just did.

"All the better," Mandingo said. "Thank you for telling me." He glanced toward the forest and frowned. "It's a shame I must share you with the others. It's rare I get one so young, so sweet."

"You will not have me if I can help it," Evelyn vowed, placing her hands flat beside her. She had made up her mind what she would do.

"There is fire in you," Mandingo said. "I like that. Some women give up before I touch them. They lie there and do nothing. You will fight me. I like that better."

"You are right. I will fight," Evelyn said, and came up out of the mud so fast, she caught him off-guard. She grabbed his ankles, heaved and sent him tumbling backward off his horse. Even as he fell, she grabbed the saddle and swung up. A smack of her hand, and his sorrel broke for the woods. She felt fingers clutch at her dress, but the mulatto could not hold on. Bending low, she glanced back.

He had risen and was taking aim.

Evelyn doubted he would shoot. What use was she to him dead? But she swung onto the side of the sorrel and hung by one arm and one leg, as her Shoshone uncle Touch the Clouds had taught her when she was barely old enough to ride. She looked back again.

Mandingo had lowered his rifle and was smiling.

Evelyn smiled, too, and then she was in the trees. Swinging up, she lashed the sorrel into a gallop. But she only went a few hundred yards, then drew rein. The smart thing to do was to keep going, to get as far from the mulatto and his friends as she could. But Dega was out there somewhere, maybe hurt, maybe dying. She had to find him. It would put her at great risk, but she refused to leave.

She reined toward the gully. That was the logical place to start. She would follow the path of mud and destruction and eventually she should find some trace of him.

Evelyn shivered. Despite the sun, she was cold. She reached up to brush a stray bang from her eyes and discovered her hair was thick with mud. She must look a sight.

The woods were ominously still.

Evelyn did not relax her vigilance for a second. The men who were after her could be anywhere. She needed a gun, needed one more than anything. The thought made her draw rein. Shifting, she opened Mandingo's saddlebags. She hoped to find a pistol or a knife, but the mulatto had all his weapons on him. "It figures," she said, and rode on.

She had a good sense of direction. She found the gully without too much trouble. But she did not get too close. The men might be watching it, too. Rising in the stirrups, she sought some sign of Dega.

The flash flood had left the gully half buried in mud and debris. When it exploded into the open, the water had spread over an area some fifty feet wide. Trees had been uprooted and tossed like matchsticks. More mud and broken trunks and torn limbs were everywhere.

Evelyn marveled that she had survived. She

feared greatly for Dega and Buttercup, and braced herself for the worst. Turning the sorrel, she paralleled the flood's path. She looked for tracks, for bodies, anything. She had been at it ten minutes when the undergrowth on the other side parted and out rode the one called Graf.

Evelyn raised her reins. She expected him to come after her, but instead he drew rein and did nothing but smirk. It made no sense. Or was it he knew he could not get across the mud quickly enough to catch her, and he did not want to spook her into riding off? He did not call out. He just stared.

Evelyn was so intent on him that she almost missed the movement to her right. A nicker from the sorrel warned her, and she turned to see Bodin moving as quietly as his horse could toward her. Already he was so close she could see the whiskers on his chin. She immediately goaded the sorrel into a trot.

"Hold on, girl!" Bodin hollered, and came after her.

Evelyn flew for her life. She was under no delusions about what they would do to her if they caught her. Across the mud, Graf paced her.

"You can't get away! You're only making it harder on yourself!" Bodin shouted.

No, Evelyn thought, she was making it harder for them. She was a good rider and could go for hours if she had to. If she were on Buttercup, she had no doubt she could eventually outdistance them. But the sorrel was not her horse. She did not know its stamina. As with people, no two horses were alike.

Bodin loved to yell. "Damn it, stop! You are making me mad!"

Evelyn counted on making him madder. On she fled, with one eye always on the mud for sign of Dega and the buttermilk. The timber became thicker, the underbrush heavier. It slowed her, but it also slowed Bodin. He did not gain any, but neither did she.

Despair nipped at Evelyn, but she fought it down. As her pa was so fond of saying, a King never gave up. She and her brother had taken that to heart. Just as they had their father's admonition that when their lives were in danger, when it was kill or be killed, they must do whatever it took to survive.

A low limb suddenly filled her vision. Evelyn ducked with mere inches to spare. Had she not seen it she would have been unhorsed. She emptied her mind and concentrated solely on riding. So far the sorrel was holding up well. She might escape yet.

Evelyn glanced back now and then. Bodin seemed content to keep her in sight. Graf was still pacing her on the other side of the mud. She noticed there was less of it, that the flood had narrowed as its force was spent, and fewer and fewer trees were uprooted. It hit her that soon they would come to the end, and Graf would close in from the side. Maybe that was what Bodin was waiting for.

Evelyn had to lose them before then. She spied a wide thicket to her right and reined toward it. Graf shouted something to Bodin, but she did not catch what it was. Without hesitating she rode straight into the thicket, knowing it would tear at her and the sorrel, but knowing, too, that it was thick and high, and that Bodin and Graf would lose sight of her. The sorrel slowed, balking. She used the reins and her legs to compel it.

Twenty feet in, Evelyn reined to the left. She bent at the waist, went another twenty feet, and drew rein.

Hooves thudded. Bodin had reached the thicket. Evelyn imagined he was trying to spot her. Unconsciously, she held her breath.

"Do you see her?" Graf hollered.

"No, damn it. Do you?"

"You're closer," Graf said.

"She has to be in this tangle," Bodin yelled. "But it must cover an acre and a half. Get over here and help me look."

"But what if my horse gets stuck in the mud?"

"Then you climb down and kick it."

Evelyn slid off the sorrel. Holding the reins, she moved toward the opposite side of the thicket, parting the brush carefully so as to make as little noise as possible. The sorrel made more, but not so much that Bodin would hear. Or so she hoped.

"Hurry it up! If she gets away it will be your fault."

"Me?" Graf replied. "What did I do? I'm coming as fast I can, but my horse keeps sinking." He swore a lurid streak, then said, "Where the hell is Mandingo, anyway? Isn't that his horse she is riding?"

"It is," Bodin shouted. "He'll have some explaining to do, and it had better be good."

Evelyn wanted them to go on yelling, but they

stopped. When she estimated she had gone about fifty feet, she moved faster. The crackle of the sorrel's passage worried her, but Bodin gave no indication that he heard.

The end of the thicket was in sight. Beyond was more timber. Once she was in among the trees, she would circle toward the gully and resume her search. There had to be some sign of Dega and Buttercup. There just had to.

Up ahead, a horse whinnied.

Evelyn's head snapped up. She smiled with joy when she beheld Buttercup. The buttermilk was layered with mud and looked done in, but appeared otherwise unhurt.

Evelyn went faster, pulling the sorrel after her, and the moment she was out of the thicket she flew to Buttercup and threw her arms around the horse's neck. "Here you are! I was so worried!"

Evelyn kissed Buttercup's muzzle and gripped the bridle. Abruptly, she saw that the reins were wrapped around a limb. Someone else had already found Buttercup and made sure she could not run off. "Dega?"

A sound drew Evelyn's gaze into the tree. Fear spiked through her. It wasn't Dega. It was Mandingo, and even as she set eyes on him, he launched himself at her.

Chapter Fourteen

Evelyn tried to whirl and run, but she had only taken a step when the mulatto slammed into her. His shoulder caught her low in the back, bowling her over. She came down hard, her senses reeling, and managed to scramble to her hands and knees. Before she could rise, a foot arced into her ribs. The pain was excruciating. She fell flat, the breath knocked out of her.

"That's for taking my horse," Mandingo said.

Evelyn looked up. He was leaning on his rifle and made no attempt to hurt her more.

"You are clever, little one. But not clever enough. You should not have stuck around."

"My friend," Evelyn gasped.

"You stayed to find him?" Mandingo said. "You a white girl and him an Indian?

"So?"

"I've lived with the hatred of whites all my life. They've treated me as if I were a diseased dog just for being part black."

Evelyn had regained some of her breath. "But you ride with whites."

"They treat me as one of them."

"They are bad men," Evelyn said.

"Spoken like a child. There is no good and bad. That is for Bible thumpers. Life is about taking what we want when we want, about always looking out for ourselves."

"If that's your outlook," Evelyn said, "I feel sorry for you."

Mandingo frowned. "I don't need your sympathy. You have not lived my life. You have not suffered as I have. I learned the hard way what counts and what does not."

"What do you and your friends intend to do with me?"

"You're not stupid. You already know."

"You're worse than bad. You are wicked. Justify it as you like, it does not change the fact that you are as low as a human being can be." Evelyn slowly sat up, pretending to be in more pain than she was.

"You have no right to judge me," Mandingo said. "You are young yet. You know nothing of the world."

"I may be young. But my folks have taught me well. I know you blame what you do on the hate whites have for you, but deep down you like it. Deep down you are scum."

Mandingo balled a fist. "You talk too much, girl. Keep it up and we will see how much talking you do without teeth."

"Brave man," Evelyn taunted. "Do you go around scaring babies, too?"

"Enough of your sass," Mandingo said, and took a step.

It was what Evelyn was waiting for. She kicked him in the knee and was rewarded with a yelp. Mandingo staggered back, limping. In a bound Evelyn reached the sorrel. She would rather take Buttercup, but Buttercup's reins were tied and she would squander precious seconds untying them. Gripping the sorrel's saddle, she went to swing up.

Behind her the thicket crackled and out hurtled Bodin astride his mount. He did not slow but galloped right at her, forcing Evelyn to let go of the saddle and leap back or be run down. As he swept past, she sprang for the sorrel again. This time she had one foot in a stirrup and was swinging her other leg up when iron arms wrapped around her waist and she was flung bodily to the ground. She rolled over, and froze. A rifle muzzle was inches from her face.

"You're a regular wildcat," Mandingo spat. "But kick me again and you'll be a dead one."

Bodin had reined around and brought his horse to a stop next to them. "I thought I heard voices," he said, climbing down.

"I caught her," Mandingo said.

"I wouldn't brag, were I you. Not unless you can explain how she got hold of your animal."

"She's tricky, this one."

"Or you're getting soft," Bodin said. "A slip of a girl, and she steals your horse, and now she nearly gets away from you a second time. I expect better of those who ride with me."

"Damn it, Bodin," Mandingo said. "She's not like other girls. She's not timid or weak."

"Next you will tell me you're scared of her," Bodin said. He turned to Evelyn. "You gave us quite a run, but it's over. You are mine now, to do with as I want. The sooner you get that through your head, the less I will have to beat on you."

"If you're smart, you will let me go," Evelyn said. "My father and my brother are looking for me."

"No parent would let their daughter traipse over these mountains with an Injun for company," Bodin said. "It was just you and him and now it is just you." He roughly hauled her to her feet. "No more of your shenanigans, hear? The next time I'll shoot you in the leg."

"You and your friends sure like to bluster," Evelyn said. But she did not resist as he shoved her toward Buttercup.

"Climb on. Try to ride off on us and I'll shoot your horse. If you think that's bluster, test me."

Again the thicket rustled, and out came Graf. "You caught her!" he crowed. "And found Mandingo, too."

"Took you long enough," Bodin said sharply. "Do you think the two of you can hold on to her now, or should I tie her?" He swung onto his horse. "Let's light a shuck. I don't like leaving Teak alone too long with those furs."

"You think he might take them for himself?" Graf asked.

"He wouldn't be that stupid," Mandingo said. "He knows we'd hunt him down."

"Never underestimate greed," Bodin said.

Evelyn held her head high. She refused to show how scared she was, refused to show weakness.

Graf was on one side of her, Mandingo on the other. Breaking away was out of the question.

Bodin looked over his shoulder. "Where did your Injun friend get to, anyway, girl?"

"The flash flood," Evelyn said sorrowfully.

"He drowned? That's too bad. I would have liked to whittle on him some. I make a game of it. I see how much they can take before they scream."

"I hope I live to watch my pa and brother kill you."

Bodin, surprisingly, laughed. "You never give up, do you? But I wasn't born yesterday. Now hush until we reach our camp."

Her despair deepening, Evelyn did something she had not done in a long time; she prayed.

The sun slowly dipped toward the horizon. In a couple of hours night would fall.

Evelyn suspected that was when they would attempt to have their way with her. She would not let them. As a last resort she intended to snatch a knife and plunge it in her heart.

Eventually they came to the clearing. Teak had a fire going and was lounging on a saddle, drinking coffee. He did not rise to greet them. "There you are. It took you nearly all damn day."

"You couldn't have done any better," Graf said.

Bodin reined up and alighted. "We're not back two seconds and already you two are bickering. I'm sick of it."

Graf began to dismount, asking, "Do we tie the girl?"

"What do you think?" Bodin snapped.

Evelyn swung a leg as if to climb down, then suddenly jabbed her heels against Buttercup harder than she had ever jabbed them before. Buttercup responded by racing straight at Bodin. He cursed and jumped out of her way. She was past him in a twinkling, and for a second she thought she would make good her escape. But Mandingo was still on his horse, and he was beside her before Buttercup could take another bound. Fingers locked in her hair. She tried to pull loose, but he was stronger. She cried out as she was wrenched into the air. It felt like her neck would snap. Then she was slammed to the ground with such force, she lay stunned, unable to move.

Bodin reached her first. "You little bitch." He rolled her over. "I should knock some sense into you, but I doubt it would do any good. Mandingo was right. You are a tricky little hellion."

Evelyn feebly resisted when Graf started to bind her wrists in front of her, but he slapped her cheek, making her ears ring, and she desisted. He dragged her near to the fire and left her lying on her side.

Teak had not moved the whole time. Taking a loud sip of coffee, he grinned at her. "Having a bad day, are we?"

"It could be better," Evelyn allowed.

"Look at the bright side," Teak said. "By tomorrow the worst will be over. You'll be dead."

Evelyn repressed a shudder. She had until dark, she imagined, until they were ready to indulge themselves.

"You are a feisty one," Teak said. "And you're

a mess. Bodin, what do you say to letting her wash up?"

"Why should I?" was the gruff rejoinder.

"She's not much to look at with all that mud on her," Teak responded. "Don't you want her pretty for the festivities?"

"I do," Mandingo said. "I like 'em pretty."

"All right," Bodin said. "But she stays tied and one of you stays close to her. If she gets away, I take it out of your hides."

Teak set down his cup and stood. "Come on, girl. The stream is just a little ways. For your own sake, don't try anything."

Evelyn slowly rose. She was stiff and sore and hurt worse than ever. Wearily, she shuffled in the direction Teak pointed, and he fell into step behind her, his rifle in the crook of his arm.

"Don't look so sad, girl. It's not as if any of this is your fault. You were just in the wrong place at the wrong time and ran into the wrong people. A lot of others have done the same and are worm food."

"You say it as if you are proud of being a killer."

"As a matter of fact, I like the stealing more than the rest of it. I'm a natural born thief. I would steal money from my folks when I was five or six."

"You were a fine son," Evelyn said.

"If you're trying to get my goat, you can stop. I won't let you make me so angry that I let down my guard, if that's your aim."

It was, but Evelyn did not admit it. "I'll tell you what I told the others. My pa or my brother or both will show up soon, and I would not want to be you when they do."

"It won't work. You can't scare me, either."

"You've never heard of Nate or Zach King?"

"Can't say as I have, no," Teak said. "And even if I had, it wouldn't make a difference. Mandingo and the others want you, and they won't be denied. I would be a fool to go against them on your behalf."

"Then you are as despicable as they are, and I have nothing else to say to you."

Teak laughed. "You have grit, I will say that. I admit I feel sorry for what you will go through, but that is as far as I will go." He paused. "I have seen how Mandingo likes to hurt them when he does it. He is an animal, that one."

The stream was before them. Evelyn sank to her knees in the grass, cupped her hands, and dipped them in the water. She raised her palms to her lips and gratefully drank.

"You are here to wash up," Teak reminded her. "I wouldn't take too long at it, either, or Bodin is liable to be mad."

"You are afraid of him, aren't you?"

"I am afraid of no man," Teak said, his voice belying his boast. "But he's fond of spilling blood, that one. He likes to kill, likes it more than anything."

"Even those who ride with him?"

"Anyone. Anywhere. Anytime." Teak glanced toward the camp. "I've been thinking of going my own way, but I must wait for the right moment. Otherwise, I'll be the one who's worm food."

Evelyn splashed water on her face. It felt good. She splashed some on her hair, but the mud was so thick, she could not remove it. Her only recourse was to plunge her whole head in and get her hair good and wet. It took several soakings before the mud loosened. Sitting back, she wrung her hair as she would a wash cloth. The water that dripped down her arms was brown. "This will take forever," she remarked.

"You're starting to look halfway human again," Teak noted.

Evelyn was in no hurry to return to the clearing. Holding her breath, she dipped her head in yet again and vigorously rubbed her hair. When she unfurled, water ran down her back and her front. She broke out in goose bumps.

"Another minute and we'll have to go back. If there is more you want to do, get it done quick."

"Yes, you're definitely scared of him," Evelyn said. "Maybe you should steal a backbone."

"Saucy little snip," Teak said. "I've treated you nice and all you do is insult me."

"If I had a weapon I would do a lot more than that."

"Enough." Teak wagged his rifle. "On your feet." A thought seemed to strike him. "Say, whatever happened to that Indian you were with?"

A lump formed in Evelyn's throat. "I wish I knew," she said softly. She imagined Dega dead, encased in a coffin of mud.

Teak poked her with the rifle. "On your feet, I said. You can mope over him later."

Evelyn began to rise. She was thinking of how

much she had liked Dega. She envisioned him standing just a few feet away, and her sorrow deepened. Then the figment of her imagination raised his lance.

"Turn, white man, and die."

Chapter Fifteen

Teak whirled and tried to bring up his rifle, but Degamawaku sprang forward and, using both hands, thrust his lance into Teak's stomach. Speared it in and up so that it sheared clear through and burst out Teak's back near his spine.

Teak stiffened and his mouth gaped wide, but the only sound that came out was a gurgle. Spittle dribbled over his lower lip, followed by a red gout. He looked at Dega in astonishment, then down at the spear embedded in his body. Mewing like a kitten, he sank to his knees, gasped, and died.

Dega pushed the body over, placed his foot on Teak's chest, and wrenched out his spear. It was covered with gore and blood, which he wiped off on the dead man's shirt.

Evelyn had been too stunned to move or speak. But now she found her voice, and with a glance through the trees toward the camp, she rose and whispered, "We have to get out of here before the others spot us." She held out her bound wrists. "Quick. Cut me free."

"I lose knife in flood," Dega said.

Evelyn hunkered next to Teak. In a sheath on his left hip was a hunting knife. Grasping it, she reversed her grip and cut at the rope.

"Let me," Dega said.

Within moments the rope was in pieces on the ground and Evelyn was helping herself to Teak's rifle and pistols. She also took his powder-horn in case the powder in her own horn was damp. She'd never had the opportunity to check.

Dega's buckskins were more brown than green, and he had mud all over his face and hair. "We kill other whites?"

"We run." Evelyn waded the stream, which only came halfway to her knees, and plunged into the vegetation on the other side. She had no doubt that within minutes Bodin and the others would be after them. "How did you find me?"

Loping at her side, Dega smiled. "I look and look after flood. Then I hear horses. I see you with those men."

"You followed us all the way here? You must be about done in."

"I tired," Dega admitted. He placed a hand on her shoulder. "I much happy you safe."

"We're not out of the woods yet," Evelyn reminded him. "Those three will not stop until they catch us or kill us."

"I not let them hurt you."

Evelyn looked at him and grew all tingly. Tearing her gaze away, she focused on running. They had to put distance between themselves and the

killers. "We need to find high ground," she said.
It would give them an edge, however slight.

"High like tree?" Dega said.

The trees. It gave Evelyn an idea. She was a fair
shot. If she could climb a tree high enough, she
might be able to pick off one or two of their pursuers. The only problem was, if she missed they
might close in before she could climb down, put-
ting her at their mercy.

"Hear that?" Dega said.

Evelyn cocked her head. Hooves drummed
from the direction of the stream, along with angry shouts. "They're after us!" She ran harder.
There would not be time to climb a tree now.

Dega stayed even with her despite a growing
pain in his side. He was bone weary and in great
pain. He had not said anything to her, but when
they were caught in the flood, a boulder had
struck him on the side as he tumbled out of control. A few of his ribs were either cracked or broken. It hurt to breathe. It hurt worse to run.

Dega remembered lying in the mud after the
flood had spent itself. Barely conscious, his chest
on fire, he had tried to rise to find Evelyn. Again
and again he made it to his hands and knees, only
to collapse. He thought he might die, so excruciating was his torment. But after a long while he
made it onto his knees, then gained his feet.
Walking had taken all he had. Every step pro-
voked more agony. But he had gritted his teeth
and kept going. Evelyn needed him; he would not
give up this side of the grave.

Much of his search he spent in a haze of pain.
He stumbled along, fading in and nearly out of

consciousness, his body mechanically perform-
ing the motions his numb brain willed. It was a
long time before the pain subsided enough for
him to feel halfway himself again.

Dega had about despaired of finding her when
he heard horses. Hoping against hope, he had
hurried toward them. His eyes had filled with
tears when he saw that she was alive. But his joy
was short-lived. To keep her in sight he had to follow them, and that meant pushing his battered
body, which in turn brought more pain.

Somehow Dega did it. Somehow he had stayed
with them. It helped that they rode at a walk. He
could not move much faster than that. His ribs
would not let him.

But now, with the renegades hard after them,
Dega would not let his condition slow him. He
would keep up with Evelyn, ribs or no ribs, pain
or no pain. Still, he could not help wincing now
and again.

"What is the matter with you?"

Dega smiled at her. "I be fine."

"Fibber." Evelyn had not noticed it until now,
but he was extremely pale and slick with sweat.
Every so often he would press his right arm to his
side and grimace. "Tell me the truth."

"It nothing," Dega insisted.

"Then why do you look like you are ready to
keel over?" Slowing, Evelyn gripped his arm.
"You're hurt, aren't you?"

Dega was thinking of the three men after them
and their guns. "Please," he urged. "We talk later."

"Now," Evelyn insisted, coming to a stop. "Or
so help me, I will not take another step."

Dega could not understand why she was making such an issue of it. Their lives were at stake. "I hurt in flood. Happy now?"

"How bad?"

"Only little hurt," Dega said.

"Is that so?" Evelyn pressed her hand to his side. Instantly, he doubled over in anguish. "I'm sorry!" she said, awash in worry. "I didn't mean to do that."

"We go," Dega said, and did so. She tugged at his sleeve, but he shrugged her off. He would not be to blame for getting them caught.

"You must rest," Evelyn urged.

"No."

"You are only making yourself worse. Please." Evelyn grabbed his arm and dug in her heels. He took a few more steps, then stopped, panting. She put her hand to his forehead. "Good Lord. You are burning with fever. You must be busted up inside. If you don't rest you could die."

"They come," Dega said.

Evelyn heard them then, heard the brush break and snap. She spun. A vague shape was coming through a belt of spruce directly behind them. The other two had spread out to each side. "Get down!" she whispered.

Dega's ribs would not be denied. He did as she wanted, but he was mad at himself. He was prepared to give his life, if he had to, to safeguard hers. "Evelyn?" he whispered.

"Yes."

"I like you."

"I like you, too."

Dega had more to say. But just then Graf appeared. He was coming toward them, the stock of his rifle resting on his leg.

Evelyn flattened, wedged Teak's rifle to her shoulder, and fixed a bead on Graf's chest. She did not want to kill him. She would as soon go her way in peace. But they would not relent. They would hunt her, however long it took, and do things to her, despicable things. She thumbed back the hammer and held her breath to steady her aim as her father had taught her.

Dega had waited for the white man to come close enough, and now he was. Shoving upright, he took a short step and threw his spear. It flashed through the air almost quicker than the eye could follow, but it was not quick enough. The spear was only halfway to its target when Graf's rifle boomed and Dega was whipped half around by a jarring blow to his shoulder.

"Dega!" Evelyn cried. She squeezed the trigger, but Graf moved as she fired.

The spear had sheared into Graf's left arm, nearly tearing him from the saddle. All his muscles served him in good stead, as, with a yank on the reins, he wheeled his mount and disappeared into the greenery.

"Who's shooting?" Bodin bellowed from off to the right.

Evelyn's legs seemed to have a mind of their own. She was up, her arm around Dega. Supporting him, she raced for their lives. He stayed with her, but he ran erratically, his legs threatening to buckle, his shoulder and chest marked by a spreading crimson stain.

"Who the hell is shooting? Someone answer me!"

Panic gnawed at Evelyn, fear Dega might die. "Can you make it?" she whispered, and he nodded. His hand was to the wound and his teeth were clenched.

From the commotion behind them, Evelyn deduced that Bodin and Mandingo were converging on Graf. It would keep them occupied a while. She went another fifty to sixty yards, until she came to a lightning-charred downed tree. Most of the limbs had broken off, but it was good cover. Sliding over the bole, she helped Dega to do the same, then said, "Sit down so I can examine you."

"We should run more," Dega objected.

"Sit."

Frowning, Dega sank with his back to the tree. He had thought the pain in his ribs was bad; the bullet wound was worse.

"Move your hand," Evelyn directed. On several occasions she had helped her mother treat gunshots, so she knew what to look for. Lightly probing with her fingers, she established that the slug had missed bone and gone clean through. Already the bleeding was slowing, which was another good sign. "It looks like you will live."

"But I weak," Dega said. "You go without me. I stay, slow them for you."

"Nothing doing," Evelyn responded. "We go together, or we do not go at all."

"You stubborn girl," Dega said. His greatest fear was not for him but for her. "You never listen."

"You have a lot to learn about females," Evelyn

countered. "Everyone says we can be contrary and everyone is right. I'm not leaving you and that is final."

"Please," Dega begged, listening for pursuit. "We not have much time."

"I know. Which is why we should not waste it arguing." Evelyn set to reloading the rifle, her fingers flying. She was not as fast at it as her father or brother, but she was no slouch, either.

Dega refused to give up. "What I do to get you go?" If they had a horse, he would throw her on it and slap it on the rump.

"And you say I am stubborn." Evelyn opened Teak's powder-horn and measured the powder in her palm.

"You want die?"

"Don't be silly. Save your breath for the fight we'll soon have on our hands."

Dega was in turmoil. Evelyn could not get it through her head how fond he was of her. "You make me want hit something."

"Uncle Shakespeare says that is what women do best. You should be flattered. If I up and left you, it would show I don't care."

That made no sense to Dega. He was so upset with her, he nearly did something the Nansusequa were trained from infancy never to do; he nearly lost his temper.

"Glare at me all you want, but you're stuck with me," Evelyn said as she slid the ramrod from its housing. "Admit it. You like it when I get your blood to boiling."

"I not like!" Dega almost exploded. "Why you not listen? Why you not see truth?"

"All I see is someone who can't take a ribbing," Evelyn teased. "Simmer down before you burst a vein."

"You—you—you are—" Dega could not find the white words. His emotions seething, he acted on impulse. He leaned forward and kissed her on the cheek.

"What was that for?"

"I angry."

"What do you do when you are mad?"

"Sorry?"

"Nothing." Evelyn tamped the ball down the barrel.

"You go now?"

"Because you kissed me?" Laughing, Evelyn shook her head. "A peck won't do it. You're stuck with me."

"I could scream," Dega said.

"Go right ahead. But they will hear you and know where we are." Evelyn leaned the rifle against the tree and drew the knife she had taken from Teak. She inserted the tip into her dress a couple of inches above the hem.

"What you do?"

"We need to bandage you and nothing else is handy." Evelyn cut in as straight a line as she could. She went all the way around so she had plenty of extra. "This might hurt a bit," she said as she eased his shoulder toward her so she could slip the bandage under his arm, and up and over.

Dega's face was so close to hers, her breath fanned his cheek. He averted his eyes, afraid of what she might see in them.

"Do you still want to bite my head off?"

"Yes."

"You are a typical male," Evelyn teased. She made a mental note to wash and clean the wound as soon as they reached water.

"I am upset male. You are pain in head."

"What a sweet thing to say."

Dega was beginning to wonder if he would ever understand her. She was so different from Nansusequa women. He started to ask her one more time to leave him, but she touched a finger to his lips.

"Shhhhh. Listen."

The killers were after them again.

Chapter Sixteen

"Get down," Evelyn said, and pressed to the earth, the rifle by her side. She could not tell whether there were two horses or three. She hoped Graf's wound had reduced the odds, but when she heard a whinny and cautiously rose up high enough to peer over the felled tree, she spied all three of them about thirty yards away roving back and forth in search of tracks. Graf's arm was in a sling made from a piece of blanket. "Darn it," she whispered.

"What?"

"We still have all three to deal with. But the good news is they have lost our sign."

"I lost spear," Dega said. "Need make new one." Without one he would be of little use to her.

"Here." Evelyn held out a pistol she had taken from Teak. "This will have to do until then."

Dega was dubious, but he accepted the gun. He had only ever fired one a few times, and he was not much good at it. He wished he had brought his bow as well as his lance.

Bodin was in a foul mood. He glared at his companions and at the ground. "They have to be around here somewhere. We're not giving up until we find them."

"They took Teak's weapons," Graf said.

"So?" Bodin snapped. "It's a girl, for God's sake. And an Injun not much more than a boy."

"That boy put a spear in me."

"You were careless. They're children, and if we can't lick them, we should give up this life and take up farming."

"I want the girl," Mandingo interjected. "She is all I have thought of since we first saw her."

Bodin swore. "Keep your mind on what we're doing or you'll end up like Graf."

"Don't worry. They won't catch *me* off-guard," Mandingo boasted.

Still arguing, they passed within a stone toss of the downed tree and rode on off into the timber.

Evelyn waited until she was sure they were out of sight and earshot, then stood. "Come on." She offered her hand to Dega.

He braced himself on the tree with his good arm and slowly rose.

"This way," Evelyn said. Sliding over the top, she headed east.

Dega slid over after her. "But pass that way," he said, pointing to the west.

"If you think I am leaving without Buttercup, you have another think coming." Evelyn had a plan. "Those three are not as smart as they think they are. They left my horse and Teak's and the two pack animals back at their camp with no one to guard them."

"What if they come back?"

"This has become cat and mouse, and on foot we are the mice. We need those horses. Once we are on horseback they will not catch us."

Dega did not share her confidence, but he admired her courage. She had an inner strength that was most uncommon. She would make a fine mate for the man who proved worthy.

Evelyn wanted to run, but she held to a walk out of worry over Dega's condition. He was still weak and burning with fever. She stopped often and made a show of listening, but she really did it so as not to tire him.

Presently, they came to the stream. Teak lay where he had fallen in a pool of drying blood.

Evelyn avoided looking at the body and hurried past. The horses had been tethered so they would not run off. "Our guardian angel is watching over us. Do you need help climbing on?"

"No," Dega said. He did not know what a guardian angel was, and would ask her later. At the moment he was finding it difficult to concentrate. The walk had exhausted him. His head was spinning. Gripping the mane of Teak's horse, he pulled himself up. He was appalled at how much effort it took. He made it, but he nearly collapsed.

"Do you need to rest?" Evelyn was watching him closely and did not like what she saw.

"I be fine," Dega lied. He refused to slow her down; he would keep up if it killed him.

Evelyn went to climb on Buttercup. She happened to glance at the pack animals, still burdened with furs, and had an inspiration. Grinning, she drew her knife and ran to them.

"What you do?" Dega asked.

"One bad turn deserves another." Evelyn cut the rope that held the furs in place on the first pack horse. All it took was a shove and they toppled to the ground. She darted to the second pack horse and spilled those furs, too. Then, laughing, she scooted back to Buttercup and climbed on.

To Dega the act seemed childish, a fit of spite that served no purpose. "All that do is make them mad."

"If that were all it would still be enough," Evelyn said. "But they will not want to leave the furs lying there in the dirt. In the time it takes them to gather the hides up, we can go another mile or two."

Dega's admiration for her rose to new heights. "You always thinking."

"Blame my pa. He made thinkers of my brother and me, although my brother tends to do his with steel and lead."

Yet another allusion Dega struggled to grasp. "You kind of woman man happy have in lodge."

"That will be the day." Evelyn gigged Buttercup. "Come on. We will circle around and head for the pass. Once we are through it, we'll be safe."

Dega had not gone far when he was covered with sweat. His shoulder throbbed. But it was his side that grew worse by the moment. His cracked or broken ribs could not take being on horseback. But he gamely rode on. It did not help that he felt as if he were burning up. After a while, though, he felt as cold as ice, and could not stop shivering.

Then he felt hot again. His vision blurred, and he shook his head to clear it.

Evelyn glanced back at him now and then. He was paler than ever, and she saw him tremble. She knew they should stop, but if they did, Bodin and the others might catch up to them. She was in a quandary as to what to do. The decision was made for her seconds later when she heard a thud.

Dega did not realize he had fallen until he felt Evelyn's hands gently rolling him onto his back. "Sorry," he breathed.

Evelyn pressed her hand to his forehead. He was hotter than before. "This is as far as we go."

"No. Leave me," Dega managed to croak.

"Not on your life. We're in this together." Evelyn picked up the pistol he had dropped and tucked it under her belt. Gazing about them, she saw a pine with boughs low to the ground. Sliding her hands under his shoulders, she attempted to boost him to his feet, but he was too heavy. So she dragged him instead. "If this hurts too much, say so and I will stop."

The pain was almost unbearable, but Dega ground his teeth and did not give in. All he could think of was what the killers would do, and it would be his fault. "Please go," he tried once more.

"Hush, will you?" Evelyn hastily made a bed of pine needles and got him to lay on his back on top of it. Then she ran to bring the horses. She figured she had two or three hours before Bodin and his friends showed up. It would give her time to prepare.

Dega struggled to stay awake. His body craved

sleep and his eyelids were heavy. He heard her sit next to him and felt her hand take his. "I lot of trouble."

"You would do the same for me," Evelyn said, and stroked his cheek. "Now I want you to lie quiet and rest. It will be dark before long. You can sleep the night through and we will head home in the morning, provided you are up to it."

"But those men—"

"You let me worry about them," Evelyn said. And she *was* worried. They were hardened cutthroats, and she was just a girl. As the saying went, she might be biting off more than she could chew, but she had to do it.

Dega had so much he wanted to say. Foremost, he desired to impress on her how sorry he was for being a burden. It tore him up inside to realize she might die because of him. "Please," he said.

"Not that again."

Dega squeezed her hand with all the strength he could muster, which wasn't much. "For me. So I not have shame."

"That is your fever talking," Evelyn replied. "You have nothing to be ashamed of. And I will not desert you."

"I like you, Evelyn."

"So you keep saying. I thank you for your friendship, but I wish you would shut up and sleep."

Dega looked at her. She did not understand. She did not understand at all. "You special," he tried again, but could say no more. He closed his eyes against the dizziness but it did not help. Despite himself, he groaned. He experienced the sensation that he was falling, but how could that be when he was lying on the ground? A black whirlpool yawned and he was powerless to resist.

Evelyn saw him go limp. "Dega?" When he did not respond, she put her ear to his chest. His heart was beating, slow but strong. "Thank God."

Standing, Evelyn untied her bedroll from her saddle, spread out a blanket, and covered Dega from his feet to his chin. Then she sat and held his hand in her lap.

She suddenly felt tired. She had been through a lot, with no rest and no food. Leaning against the pine, she gazed down at Dega, drinking in his handsome face. She ran the tip of a finger along his eyebrow and smiled at her boldness. "What am I going to do with you?" she asked softly. "Why have you come into my life?"

They were questions she had asked herself many times in the past several weeks. Questions she could not answer.

Buttercup nickered. It reminded Evelyn she had a lot to do before their enemies arrived. Since it was just her now, she must rely on her wits more than ever.

Evelyn rose to her knees and began scooping pine needles onto the blanket. She covered it completely, then sprinkled needles on his forehead, chin and neck. Stepping back, she surveyed her handiwork and nodded in satisfaction. From a distance he would blend into the ground.

"I hope you live," Evelyn said. Then, taking hold of the reins of both horses, she led them back the way they had come, a good fifty yards, and tied them to trees. She stroked and kissed

Buttercup, saying, "You have been the best horse I ever owned."

Evelyn faced to the north. That was the direction Bodin and the others would come from. She hiked for several minutes, searching all the while for a suitable spot to make her stand.

She was under no illusion about the outcome. Three against one. They were proficient at taking life and she was not. So far, luck had seen her through, but her luck would not hold forever.

A large spruce seemed as likely a tree as any. Making sure both pistols were tight under her belt, Evelyn held the rifle by the barrel, and climbed. The limbs were close together and would screen her from scrutiny. She settled with her back to the bole and her legs wrapped around a thick branch.

From her vantage, Evelyn could see a considerable way. She was nervous, and growing more so. She did not want to die. She was young yet, and there was much she had not seen and done that she would like to. She thought of her mother and father and how loving they were, and of her brother and how dearly she cared for him even though he could be such a pain. She thought of how when she was younger, her father would sit at the table most nights and read to them while their mother rocked in the rocking chair by the fire, sewing or darning. She recalled the fun times they'd had, the picnics they went on, the long rides for the pleasure of riding, the weeks each summer they spent with the Shoshones.

"I have had a good life," Evelyn said to herself.

In the distance a pair of ravens cawed and took wing.

Evelyn checked the rifle and pistols. She turned the pistols so the butts faced outward for a cross draw. She loosened the knife in its sheath.

A doe and two fawns came bounding out of the undergrowth. They stopped and the doe looked back. Her ears erect, she gave a snort. Mother and young were soon out of sight.

Evelyn craned her neck but did not see them yet. It would not be long. She held out her right hand and scowled. Her fingers were shaking. Making a fist, she shook it.

"You can do this. You are a King, and you can do this."

She envied her brother. He could kill without a qualm. Even as a boy, his sole ambition was to count coup. He had always looked forward to the day he would be a full-fledged warrior.

Sparrows took wing, chirping excitedly.

Evelyn tensed.

There they were, all three of them, spread out twenty yards apart. Bodin was in the middle, Mandingo on the right, Graf the left. They had their eyes on the ground.

Taking a deep breath, Evelyn let it out slowly. It seemed to help.

"Here is a track!" Mandingo hollered. "We're getting close."

"Whoever sees the boy first, kill him," Bodin said. "Then we will treat ourselves to the girl."

"She has given us more trouble than anyone, ever," Graf commented.

"All the more reason we can't let her get away," Bodin said. "No snip of a female gets the better of us."

Evelyn wedged the rifle to her shoulder and aligned the rear sight with the front sight and centered the bead on Bodin's chest.

"God help me," she said.

Chapter Seventeen

Evelyn King was set to squeeze the trigger when the three killers unexpectedly stopped. Mandingo had said something to Bodin, something she did not quite catch. Then, to her considerable surprise, the mulatto reined to the east and trotted off. Bodin and Graf stayed where they were.

Evelyn did not know what to make of it. She lowered the rifle and waited. She did not want to shoot anyone if she could help it. She hoped, she prayed, that they would simply go away.

The minutes dragged. The shadows lengthened. The sun, perched on the western horizon, would soon relinquish its reign.

The two men sat on their horses and did nothing. They did not even talk.

Evelyn kept looking for Mandingo to return, but there was no sign of him. It could be a blessing in disguise, she mused. If he did not get back before dark, they would have to wait until morning to resume the hunt. That would give her time to spirit Dega away.

Bodin chose that moment to rein his mount over to Graf.

Evelyn leaned out as far as she dared, but she could not hear what they were saying. She shifted to relieve a cramp in her leg, but it would not go away. She glanced at the sun, now half gone. In a little while she could climb down.

The wind picked up. The tree gave a slight shake and she instinctively clutched a limb above her.

Not once had Bodin or Graf glanced in her direction. They were both grinning.

Evelyn wondered what they were so happy about. Teak was dead, Graf was wounded, and she and Dega had escaped. By rights they should be as mad as could be. She looked to the east and saw only trees.

Suddenly Bodin drew a pistol. Evelyn tensed, but he did not point it at her. He aimed it to the north, and fired. For the life of her, she could not figure out what he shot at. It appeared to be a tree. But why in heaven's name would he indulge in target practice? she wondered.

Then, compounding her puzzlement, Graf did the exact same thing.

Bewildered, Evelyn tilted her head to try and hear snatches of their conversation. In doing so, she glanced down—straight into the savagely gleeful face of Mandingo a few feet below her.

For all of five seconds, Evelyn was frozen in shock. A hand on her ankle galvanized her to life. She tried to bring the rifle to bear but she was too slow. Mandingo twisted her leg and pulled, and before Evelyn could stop herself, she was plummeting to earth. She crashed onto a branch, grabbed at another but missed, and struck a third. The rifle went flying.

The ground rushed up to meet her. Pain spiked her shoulder, and she came close to passing out. Dimly, she heard the rapid drum of hooves. Shapes loomed over her, and someone relieved her of the pistols and the knife.

Gradually, things acquired form and substance. Evelyn blinked up into the cruel countenances of the three killers. They ringed her, making flight impossible.

"Can you hear me, girl?" Bodin asked.

Evelyn swallowed her fear. "Yes."

"Can you move or did the fall break something?"

Propping herself on an elbow, Evelyn took stock. She moved both arm and both legs and turned her head from side to side. "I appear to be in one piece."

"Good," Bodin said. "You wouldn't be much fun if you weren't." He turned and clapped Mandingo on the shoulder. "That was damn clever. She never suspected."

"How did you know I was up there?" Evelyn wanted to know.

"I saw the sunlight gleam off your rifle barrel," Mandingo explained. "I told the others to wait while I circled around, and to make noise when they saw me climb the tree."

Evelyn had never felt so stupid as she did at that moment. "I should have shot at you when I had the chance."

"Where is your Injun friend?" Bodin asked.

"I don't know. We became separated. He must be miles away by now."

"What about the two horses? Did he take them and leave you here by your lonesome?"

"I made him go. He was hurt," Evelyn said. "I stayed behind to buy him time to get away."

"I'm not that gullible," Bodin said. "I told you before and I will tell you again. You are a terrible liar." Lunging, he gripped the front of her dress and yanked, forcing her to sit up. "Now what say we stop playing games? Answer honest or you will suffer. Where's the Injun?"

"I told you, I don't know."

"Suit yourself," Bodin said. Hauling her to her feet, he shoved her against Graf, who in turn shoved her against Mandingo. She tried to leap clear, but Mandingo held on to her arms.

"This is going to hurt you a lot more than it will hurt us," Bodin remarked.

Evelyn never saw the punch. She felt it, though, felt the torment in her stomach, and bitter bile rise in her gorge. Doubling over, she tottered.

"There's more where that came from," Bodin warned. "Unless you're fond of pain, you better start cooperating."

Graf seized her wrist. "Let me have her for half an hour. I'll make her talk."

Mandingo grabbed her other wrist. "No. Bodin promised her to me if I caught her. I'll make her tell us what we want to know."

"Quit your damned squabbling," Bodin snapped. "I swear, sometimes you two are worse than women."

The next moment the brush parted and out

shambled an apparition in green buckskins caked with mud and covered with pine needles. In Dega's right hand was a two-foot length of broken tree limb. "Let go of her!"

"Shoot him," Bodin said to Graf.

"No!" Evelyn cried. She went to move between them, but Mandingo held her fast.

Graf drew his other pistol. "Killing Injuns is always a pleasure." He took deliberate aim.

Evelyn could not stand there and do nothing. She fought to break free, but Mandingo was too strong. She braced for the crack of Graf's flintlock, but he did not shoot. There was no need.

Dega had collapsed in an unconscious heap.

"Will you look at that?" Bodin said. "He's about done in."

"I knew I hit him earlier," Graf declared. "A little lower, and he would've bled to death."

"Let me go to him," Evelyn pleaded.

"Sorry, girl," Bodin replied. "You're ours now. But if it will make you feel better, we'll drag him back to camp and carve on him while you watch. How would that be?"

"To call you a beast would insult the beasts," Evelyn said bitterly.

Bodin laughed. "That spunk of yours has served you well. For what it's worth, you have earned my respect."

"Respect from scum is no respect at all."

Mandingo let go of her and stepped back. "You will ride with me. Behave or the boy dies that much sooner."

Evelyn did not hesitate. She was not going to let them do what they intended. A fate worse than death, as it was called, was truly a fate worse than death, in her estimation.

She sprang at Bodin, raking his face with her fingernails while simultaneously grabbing at his knife with her other hand. He howled in rage as her nails dug deep. The hilt of the knife molded to her palm and she swept it out. The tip was a whisker from slicing into his belly when her arm was seized by Mandingo and nearly torn from its socket. She clawed at his face, but Graf clamped his hand on her other wrist. Desperate to break free, she kicked at their knees.

Bodin punched her. He gave no warning. He sank his fist into her gut and drew his fist back to do it again.

The pain doubled Evelyn over. Wheezing and gagging, she sagged and would have fallen if the other two had not been holding her.

"Damn you," Bodin snarled. "You nearly took my eye out." He touched a finger to the scratch marks and stared at the drops of blood. "For this you will take a long time dying."

Evelyn felt Mandingo's grip on her arm tighten. She glanced up, thinking Bodin was about to do something, but he was not even looking at her; he was staring past her, his rat face mirroring surprise. Mandingo and Graf had shifted and were also staring at something behind her. Still unable to straighten, she glanced over her shoulder—and came close to bursting into tears.

Two newcomers had materialized as if out of the thin mountain air. One was a giant in buckskins, with raven hair and a black beard. His green eyes seemed to blaze with inner fire and his features were set in grim lines. He held a Hawken rifle at his side.

The second man was smaller. He was a mix of white and red, his face similar enough to that of the giant to show they were blood kin. He was clean-shaven. His dark eyes did not blaze like those of his father, but there was an aura of menace about him, an air of raw savagery about to be unleashed.

"Who the hell are you two?" Bodin demanded. "This is a private matter. You will fan the breeze if you know what is good for you."

Evelyn found her voice. "Good to see you again, Pa."

"We came as quick as we could," Nate King said.

Bodin took a step back. "Oh hell."

"The other one is my brother, Zach," Evelyn told him. "Even though you have treated my friend and me badly, I am sorry for what is about to happen to you."

Mandingo and Graf released her and moved to either side.

"Evelyn," Nate said. "Go over by Dega."

No one tried to stop her. Evelyn knelt and cradled Dega's head on her knees. "Whenever you're ready, Pa."

Graf gave a nervous cough. "There are three of us and only two of them."

Zach King had his rifle in one hand. With the other he slowly slid a tomahawk from under his brown leather belt. "Three or ten, it would not make a difference."

"Is that so, boy?" Bodin sneered. "We are not sheep. You'll not find us easy."

Zach was staring at Mandingo. "I am Stalking Coyote of the Shoshone. I have counted coup on Sioux. I have counted coup on Blackfeet and Bloods. I have counted coup on Piegans. I have killed whites, and breeds, and every animal that lives in these mountains. And now, for what you have done to my sister, I am going to kill you."

And just like that, he leaped at Mandingo. The mulatto tried to skip out of reach while bringing his rifle up, but the tomahawk opened his shoulder.

Graf tried to draw his pistol. He did not quite have it clear when Nate King's Hawken boomed. The heavy-caliber slug smashed Graf back onto his heels. He swayed and bleated, "This can't be!" Then he pitched forward, dead.

Bodin turned and ran.

Evelyn flung out her arm, tripping him. Before he could scramble to his feet, her father was on him, lifting him as if he were a sack of flour and landing a blow that she would have sworn nearly caved in Bodin's skull. Her father stripped Bodin of his pistols, then gave him a push. Bodin staggered back, clawing at his knife. Her father drew his bowie.

A flurry of movement diverted Evelyn's attention to Zach and Mandingo. The mulatto had dropped his rifle and resorted to his long knife. He was grinning, maybe because he was good with a blade and confident of his ability. But his grin soon died. For although he cut and thrust and stabbed with lighting speed, every move was countered or evaded or blocked. She could see the truth begin to dawn on him, and the first inkling of fear.

Evelyn could have told him. No one knew her brother better than she did. No one could appreciate what her brother was capable of. Among the Shoshones, only Touch the Clouds had counted more coup. Mandingo was a killer, but he was not half the killer her brother was.

As if to bear her out, Zach took a step back. "I am done toying with you," he said. "Sis, you might not want to look."

Mandingo crouched and moved his knife in a circle. "When I am done with you I will have my way with her."

Zach became a blur.

Evelyn could not quite follow it all. Mandingo lanced his knife at her brother's chest, but Zach sidestepped and slashed his tomahawk across the mulatto's thigh. Blood spurted, and Mandingo nearly fell. He stabbed high, but Zach wasn't there. The tomahawk streaked once, twice, three times, and Mandingo looked down at the stump where his hand and the knife had been.

"No!"

"Yes," Zach said, and sheared the tomahawk into Mandingo's crotch. Mandingo threw back his head and screamed. He probably never saw the tomahawk arc up and across. It severed most of his neck from his body.

Zach stared at the twitching ruin and said, "That was for my sister."

Evelyn had almost forgotten about her father. She turned, and gasped. He was standing over Bodin, who was sprawled on his back. The bowie had opened Bodin from his waist to his sternum, and his organs were oozing out.

Her eyes welling up with tears, Evelyn bowed her head and gave thanks. Then her father and brother were by her side, her father holding her and comforting her. She looked at her brother and was amazed to see tears in his eyes, too. "Thank you," she said softly.

Zach coughed, and smiled. "We can't leave you alone for two minutes, can we, without you getting into trouble?"

"Dega," Evelyn said to her father. "He was shot. He has a fever."

Nate examined him. He undid the bandage and studied the flesh around the wound, even going so far as to sniff it. "He will live, daughter."

"You're sure, Pa?"

"There is no sign of infection. I have some of your mother's herbs in my parfleche. We will rest a day or two and I will treat him, then we will rig a travois for him to lie on and head home."

"Home," Evelyn said. The word never sounded so good.

NIGHT HAWK

STEPHEN OVERHOLSER

He came to the ranch with a mile-wide chip on his shoulder and no experience whatsoever. But it was either work on the Circle L or rot in jail, and he figured even the toughest labor was better than a life behind bars. He's got a lot to learn though, and he'd better learn it fast because he's about to face one of the toughest cattle drives in the country. They've got an ornery herd, not much water and danger everywhere they look. The greenhorn the cowboys call Night Hawk may not know much, but he does know this: The smallest mistake could cost him his life.

ISBN 10: 0-8439-5840-5
ISBN 13: 978-0-8439-5840-9

HEADING WEST
Western Stories
NOEL M. LOOMIS

Noel M. Loomis creates characters so real it's hard to believe they're fiction, and these nine stories vividly demonstrate his brilliant storytelling talent. Within this volume, you'll meet Big Blue Buckley, who proves it takes a "Tough *Hombre*" to build a railroad in the 1880s and "The St. Louis Salesman" who struggles with the harsh terrain of the Texas prairie. Most poignant of all is the dying Comanche warrior passing on the ways of his people in "Grandfather Out of the Past," a tale that won Loomis the prestigious Spur Award. Each story sweeps you back in time to the Old West as it really was.

ISBN 10: 0-8439-5897-9
ISBN 13: 978-0-8439-5897-3

To order a book or to request a catalog call:
1-800-481-9191
This book is also available at your local bookstore, or you can check out our Web site **www.dorchesterpub.com** where you can look up your favorite authors, read excerpts, or glance at our discussion forum to see what people have to say about your favorite books.

MAX BRAND®

TWISTED BARS

He was known as The Duster. Five times he'd been tried for robbery and murder, and five times acquitted. He'd met the most famous of gunmen and beaten them all. Before he gives it all up, he's got one battle left to fight. The Duster needs a proper burial for his dead partner, but the blustery Rev. Kenneth Lamont refuses to let a criminal rest in his cemetery. The Duster knows if he can't get what he wants one way, there's always another. And this is a plan the reverend won't like. Not one bit...

ISBN 10: 0-8439-5871-5
ISBN 13: 978-0-8439-5871-3

To order a book or to request a catalog call:
1-800-481-9191
This book is also available at your local bookstore, or you can check out our Web site **www.dorchesterpub.com** where you can look up your favorite authors, read excerpts, or glance at our discussion forum to see what people have to say about your favorite books.